CARNIVALS AND CORPSES

A MIRA MICHAELS MYSTERY

JULIA KOTY

BUSSTOP PRESS

1

———————

The bright sun of the June afternoon reflected off the chrome detailing on the outside of the Soup and Scoop diner. The iridescent blue of the siding gleamed like car's paint.

Aerie locked the entrance door. "You're going to love the flea market, Mira. And the carnival is so much fun."

We had double-timed the cleanup to get out early, and I had run home to grab my dog. Today was one of the largest openings for the local flea and farmer's market. "I'm excited to find some fresh produce and fruits for the diner." A traveling carnival had come to town yesterday, and since it was situated right next to the farmer's market, we were going to check out both.

"I can finally show you some of my favorite things about summertime in Pleasant Pond." Aerie and I had been very busy with the diner. As the weather had warmed, we ended up with more people visiting us for lunch and take-out.

Ozzy barked at my feet. She was ready for a walk and a flea market adventure. Arnold, my cat, had literally told me to take the dog out to give him some peace and quiet. My old

Victorian house was quite rowdy these days—if Arnold had his way, I would have taken Taco the macaw with his colorful language, and the two giant Koi fish I had recently acquired, to sell at the flea market. I grinned. "I wonder whether there will be any organic pet feed at the market. I also need some fresh fruit to experiment with new ice cream recipes." Ice cream was now the most popular item on the menu.

Aerie had mentioned the flea market to me a while back, but this would be my first time attending and I was excited to see what we would find.

"Where is this place again?" I belted my overly excited pup into the backseat. "Sit, Ozzy."

"It's where the old drive-in movie theater used to be."

"You forget I didn't grow up here." I was raised in New England but had happily found a new home here in Pennsylvania.

"It's about a mile behind the high school."

I nodded. The town of Pleasant Pond covered a large area of open acres of land all adjacent to its namesake.

My ancient gray Buick, Babs, had been acting up. As soon as I had a few more dollars in my bank account, I'd take her in to be serviced. In the meantime, I was glad Aerie agreed to drive. There was no need for us to get stranded at the farmer's market. It would be hard to carry all the produce the few miles home.

No sooner had I put on my seatbelt than she leaned conspiratorially over to me. "So, Mira, what's the deal with you and Dan?" She winked as she pulled out onto Main Street.

"Focus on the driving. There's nothing going on between me and Dan."

"Not from where Sam and I were sitting. You guys were getting pretty cozy during the movie last week."

"I don't know what you're talking about. All I remember is some spilled popcorn and when I happened to choke on a kernel, Dan offered me a sip of his soda."

"I knew it! You called him Dan instead of Detective Lockheart." She nodded. "You've got it bad."

I turned my whole body in the seat and stared at her. "You have got to be kidding me. I can't call somebody by their first name without you inferring some deep relationship?"

"Not from you."

"What is that supposed to mean?"

"You've always acted weird around Dan. And I always wondered why." She grinned. "But now I know."

"Know what? Nothing is going on."

"Fight me all you want. The truth is the truth." She bubbled with laughter. "Well, we're here."

I glanced around surprised. "Really?"

"Yeah, I told you this town is so small everything is next to everything else."

We passed an ancient drive-in movie screen. It stood like a giant aging white billboard and some brave souls had climbed to its corner and spray-painted it with graffiti.

On the grounds where cars would normally park for a movie were rows and rows of vendors with folding tables and gimmicky signs hawking their wares. I couldn't wait. I also desperately wanted to get away from the "Dan" conversation.

I hopped out of the car as soon as she set the emergency brake. The summer sun was hot, but a cool breeze blew across the field and fluttered through my shirt, lifting the sweaty tank top from my back.

The rows of tables in front were set up for the farmer's market. Bright red cherries caught my eye lying on the closest table. The idea of an almond cherry ice cream popped into my head and I just had to have them. I opened the door to the backseat and grabbed Ozzy on her leash and the reusable shopping bags Aerie kept there. It was time to go shopping.

Aerie walked around her car with a grin on her face. "You look like a kid in a candy store."

"I feel like one. Do you see those cherries?"

"There are some strawberries over there. I'm thinking of a vegan strawberry tart." She rubbed her hands together. We made our way to the tables and the grinning faces of the local farmers. A woman gently packed five pounds of cherries in my bag and glanced up at me, saying, "Another month and we will have honey crisp apples, and then after that we'll have more varieties." The idea of apple crisp made my mouth water. "We have pick-your-own starting at the very end of August. Here's our flyer, and you can find us online." She added a flyer to my bag and handed it to me.

"Thank you." I took my bag gratefully, already plotting out the future recipe for the cherry almond ice cream. Maybe I would even boil down some cherries to make a syrup. I looked around and found Aerie where I expected, near the last strawberries of the season. "Hey Aerie, I see that farmer Miller has fresh eggs. Would you like to get some for the diner?"

"You're the chef. You know what our customers want." I had only been chef for a couple months. But Aerie enjoyed giving me full rein. "Besides," she said, "I like the idea of supporting Mr. Miller as part of our community."

I balanced the bag of cherries and the leash while

shaking open a second shopping bag. "Hi, Mr. Miller. Could I have three dozen of your eggs?"

"Buying for the diner?"

"Of course; only the best for our customers." I fumbled with the bag until Mr. Miller offered to open it for me.

He gently placed three cartons of eggs inside and I paid him probably half of what organic eggs cost up north.

"You two should head to the flea market. My cousin is there selling some of the antiques he picked up at an auction. He's over there in the blue baseball cap with the dolphin on the front. You just tell him Mike sent you."

"Thanks, Mr. Miller." I hooked the bag of eggs on my elbow and glanced in the direction of the flea market. It looked like a wonderland of random treasures.

"We could put all of this in the car and then browse," Aerie suggested. "I can open up the windows. There is a bit of a breeze. If we're quick I don't think we have to worry too much."

The weight of five pounds of cherries and three-dozen eggs wasn't exceptionally heavy, but they were on the fragile side, and Ozzy deserved a good walk. If we put it away, we could scan through the flea market faster. "Okay, let's go."

After putting all of our produce and eggs in the car in the most shaded area we could, Aerie rolled down the windows to get some ventilation. We'd only explore for a few minutes—the food would be fine. I hoped.

"C'mon Ozzy, let's find a treasure." I was super excited to check out the flea market.

Ozzy tugged on her leash as Aerie and I wandered down the rows of tables covered in everything from purses and jewelry to antique farming implements. If you were looking for something obscure, I imagine you could find it here, along with something as practical as a paring knife. I was still on the hunt for furniture for my house. Anything cheap that was still functional. Aerie had stopped at a table full of jewelry, handmade bracelets, earrings, necklaces, and beads.

"Isn't this pretty?" She held up a tiny silver teardrop-shaped cage. On closer inspection it held beach glass in different shades of blue and green. "It's gorgeous."

While Aerie paid for her new find, I walked farther down the aisle, spotting a desk I could definitely put to good use at home. I already imagined it sitting in the corner of my living room. The seller had an airstream parked behind the table full of the odds and ends that you would find in a grandma's attic.

As luck would have it, the proprietor was a man wearing a blue baseball cap with a dolphin on the front, Mike Miller's cousin. He was sweating profusely, and he looked a little preoccupied. I examined the desk. It appeared to have been recently stained in a warm golden color so the beautiful wood grain showed through the layer of shiny lacquer.

It was an old style rolltop desk, and when I pulled, the slatted cover gave a satisfying click as each slat unfolded and connected smoothly with the desktop. I opened it back up and peeked into the tiny drawers on top.

"I'll sell that to you for cheap," said Mike's cousin.

I walked around the desk. It appeared to be in great shape. "How much do you want for it?" I needed to know if this was going to be too rich for my blood, because pretty much everything was these days.

"How much are you willing to pay?"

"I doubt I have enough for this. It's beautiful."

He nodded curtly. "Name your price."

"Forty bucks?" It was all that I had in the pocket of my

phone. This antique rolltop desk had to be worth at least ten times that amount.

"It's yours." He held out his hand. I laid two twenties in his calloused palm. He furtively glanced around and stuffed the twenties in his pocket instead of the lockbox that sat at his table. He saw me notice it and slammed the box shut, twisted the key, stuffing the key into his pocket.

"I have to go. Enjoy the desk." He ducked through the crowd. I watched as he snatched his hat off his head. Immediately, he was lost in the shuffle of people.

Aerie came up behind me. "Is that yours?"

I turned back to the desk. "It appears so." I ran a hand along the top of its smooth lacquered surface. "I bought it from Mike Miller's cousin. But he ran off."

"What do you mean he ran off?" A breeze pulled strands of her golden hair from its elastic.

"He slammed shut his lockbox, took the key with him, and disappeared into the crowd."

"Maybe he had to use the facilities." Aerie glanced in the direction of the bathrooms and shivered. She had a thing about outhouses and porta-potties.

"Yeah. Maybe." I looked around his table area. No one else seemed to be with him. I couldn't imagine anyone leaving their lockbox full of cash unattended, even if they had to use the restroom. He had been acting strangely. I walked behind the table.

Aerie gave me a look. "What are you doing?"

"Something doesn't feel right. He let me buy that desk for next to nothing and he was acting very strange. Then he disappears without the rest of the money? Something's up."

"I wish I had seen him. Maybe his aura would have given us a clue. I've been practicing reading auras. Oh—maybe we should call Detective Lockheart. See what he thinks." Even

Aerie's needling me about Dan didn't distract me from trying to figure out what seemed so wrong with this situation. Sometimes things just felt wrong to me and I was learning it usually meant a mystery was brewing.

The table was covered with a clean yellow tablecloth and a wide selection of antiques, a beat-up wooden music box, a cardboard container of books, random dishes and teacups.

"Ordinary stuff for a flea market table." Ozzy pulled on her leash as she walked around sniffing the table legs.

Aerie scrutinized the offerings. "Nothing odd or out of place?"

"I don't see anything."

I ducked under the table and found a large red and white cooler. I pried up the lid. Immediately Ozzy's nose joined me at the cooler. A zip-topped bag holding two sandwiches and a six-pack of lime soda sat on top of a bed of ice. "Just his lunch." I closed the lid. Ozzy jumped back down and sniffed around hoping to find the scent of a new friend to play with, so I held tight to her leash.

As soon as I stood up Aerie gave me a nod in the direction of the table next to us. "Right."

A middle-aged woman completed the sale of a hand-knit ribbed hat. She sat back down and picked up her knitting project.

"Excuse me?" I leaned in her direction.

"Can I help you?" She continued to knit even though her eyes were trained on me.

"Do you know the man who sells at this table? Blue baseball cap?"

Her smile was conciliatory. "No, sorry, I'm new. This is the first year I'm selling at the flea market."

"You didn't get a chance to talk to him at all?"

"No. I've been a bit busy between sales and my project." She lifted her needles up with the knitted green strands of yarn dangling.

"Okay, thanks." Ozzy tugged hard on the leash.

Aerie walked back over from the table across the crowded fairway. "Any luck?"

"No, she says she didn't know the guy and didn't see anything out of the ordinary."

"We can talk to Mr. Miller; he did mention that this is his cousin." Aerie put her hand on her hip. "Do you really have that feeling? I mean maybe he just went to the bathroom or had to make a private phone call or something."

I shrugged. I did have a gut feeling that told me something was wrong, but Aerie was right. There was nothing to go on. Ozzy tugged on her leash and whined. "I guess we can go. My spidey-sense is just overreacting." I pulled on the leash. "Come on, Ozzy, let's go."

She resisted my tug and whined again. She stood on her hind legs scratching at the wheel well of the airstream trailer parked behind the table. I squatted down to her eye level. "What's up, Ozzy? Come on, we'll go home and get you some treats."

And then I smelled what was making her antsy. Blood. My eyes adjusted to the dark shadow underneath the airstream. That's when I saw the body. I jumped up.

"Well then, I guess we will be calling Dan after all." I put my hand on the table to steady myself and tried not to hyperventilate.

"What? What did you see? Did you have, like, a vision?"

"I am not my sister. I'm not a psychic. There is a body under that airstream."

"Oh my gosh, serious?" It always amazed me how excited Aerie got about anything out of the ordinary. She stepped around the table and went down on her hands and knees to stare into the shadows under the trailer. "Oh boy." She slowly stood and pulled her cell phone out of her back pocket. "I'll call him."

I nodded in agreement. For some reason I always happened to be on the scene of whatever new murder happened to occur in our town. Not too long-ago, Detective Dan Lockheart had put me in a jail cell for asking too many questions. I sighed. The last thing he needed was to see was me at a murder scene.

2

The afternoon sun glared on the airstream's silver, domed-pill shape. "We should take a look inside."

Aerie's eyes lit up. "You know that's breaking and entering, right?"

I gave her a shrug with a smile. She grinned back. We had done this before. "You keep watch." I handed her Ozzy's leash.

She frowned. "Next time I get to go."

"Let's not keep hoping for next times." But I had to admit, all the mysteries we solved had given me the sleuthing bug. I couldn't *not* look in the trailer. I turned the handle to the door and quickly stepped into the airstream. I shut the door behind me. The heat was suffocating. After being out in the bright sunshine, I could barely see my hand in front of my face. It smelled stuffy, like old laundry, and the temperature was unbearably hot. I felt like I was in a slow cooker. My mind went a different direction and hoped the cherries and eggs weren't feeling the same way in Aerie's car.

The outlines of furniture slowly came into focus as my

eyes adjusted. A table with magazines about antiques on it. A stool. A dirty breakfast dish. I had to be quick, I couldn't let Detective Lockheart find me in here. I'd end up in jail again. I shimmied my way around the room trying not to move or touch anything. A closed laptop lay on the counter connected to the wall by its charger. My fingers itched to open it and poke around, but I knew I couldn't leave prints. Next to it was a printer with a single piece of paper sitting in the output tray. I couldn't help myself. I picked it up, anxious for a clue. Blank. I put it back hoping the police wouldn't dust for fingerprints on a piece of blank paper. A loud knock sounded on the door.

"I hear sirens," Aerie warned.

I ducked out of the airstream, squinting in the bright sun, but thankful for the fresh air.

Aerie and I kept it quiet about the body until Dan arrived a few minutes later. Once he got there with additional police officers, things got exciting.

After directing his officers, Detective Lockheart made a beeline in our direction. "Why am I not surprised to see you here?"

Aerie immediately jumped to my defense. "Seriously Dan, we were simply shopping at the flea market."

"Just the luck of being in the wrong place at the wrong time, every time?" The corner of Dan's mouth turned up slightly as he looked at me.

"If I had my choice, I'd be over at the carnival eating fried dough," I said. I gathered Ozzy into my arms so she would stop whining. Plus, it's a well-known fact that holding a pet makes you totally look less suspicious. I felt guilty about checking out the trailer and hoped the guilt wasn't on my face.

"You were shopping? You bought something from this table?"

"Yeah, I bought that desk. The guy that sold it to me; we think he's Mr. Miller's cousin. He sold the desk to me very cheaply and he seemed to be in a rush, then he ran off without his lockbox." I pointed to the grey metal box that sat on the table's edge.

My phone rang. I automatically pressed the side and silenced it while it was still in my pocket.

"Mr. Miller's cousin? Are you sure? You didn't get his name?"

"No." I stared at the desk wondering if it was even his to sell. My mind went over everything that happened again to try to put the pieces together.

"I'll be sure to talk with Mr. Miller." Dan wrote in his notebook before glancing up at me. "*You* do not need to question Mr. Miller. *You* do not need to do anything about this case. Is that clear?"

This is exactly why Aerie is completely off when she talks about Dan and me getting together. Because I absolutely hated when he told me what to do. Or what not to do. I no longer felt guilty about snooping, I felt angry, so angry. Like on some other level I can't even explain, but my ears got hot and I wanted to tell him I could do anything I wanted. Including talking with Mr. Miller about his cousin. But before I could get a word out my phone rang again. This time I turned the phone over and looked at it. The call was from Darla. My psychic sister. That's all I needed. I had been avoiding her two-cent psychic opinions about my life since I moved here. But she always seemed to know when something was up.

"Hello."

"It's me."

"Yeah, I know. My phone says so. I don't have time right now to chat." She always called at the most inopportune times. And always tried to run my life.

"Okay, okay, but I'm at the diner. Which house is yours?"

"You're where?" I put Ozzy on the ground.

"I'm at the diner. It's closed, by the way. Where are you?"

"Never mind where I am. Why are you here?"

"That's too big of an explanation for a phone conversation, isn't it?"

"Just stay put. I'll be there in five minutes."

Aerie took Ozzy's leash from my hand as I punched end-call on my phone and jammed it into my back pocket.

"We have produce in the car anyway so we need to go." I pivoted on my heel to walk away, but Aerie stopped me and turned to Dan. "It was nice seeing you, Dan."

Dan nodded and waved in an attempt to catch my attention, but I ignored him. I had bigger fish to fry. Why in the world was my sister here?

Ozzy sat in my lap on the way back to the diner. She was as happy as ever to be on a car ride. I wasn't so content. I took a deep breath.

Aerie attempted a quick glance at me. "So, your sister is in town?" There was an edge of excitement to her voice. I knew Aerie was a bit of a fan of my sister. My sister's famous reputation definitely preceded her wherever she went.

"Yes. But I've told her a million times not to visit me. Independence is not having your older sister show up unannounced."

"Maybe there's a family emergency?"

"The emergency is that she needs to get back in her car and go home."

"Doesn't your sister live in Massachusetts?"

I knew what she was hinting at. I couldn't send my sister right back to another eight-hour drive. She would have to stay.

"Can she stay at your house?" I blurted.

"You know I would say yes. After all, she is Darla Damien. But Jay is back living at the house, and well, Sam comes over..." She trailed off, hinting at the idea of an additional guest not being a good one.

Sam was Aerie's boyfriend. He ran the pizza shop at the edge of town. Best pizza ever. But I understood what she meant. I had to deal with my sister. Just like she had to deal with Jay moving in and out of the house because of his crazy girlfriend, Chelsea.

"It's fine. I'll figure something out." I was so irritated at my sister, but I didn't need to put Aerie out. I just wished my sister would go home and stay out of my life.

Once we turned onto Market Street, I could see her Rio-green Studebaker parked in front of the diner. My heart stuttered in my chest. I'm not generally afraid of confrontation, but my sister is an entirely different matter. She has mothered me most of my life and smothered me as well. Good intentions aside, every time she had a psychic vision involving me, she felt the need to share. Which always forced my hand into doing the opposite. Thus, completely screwing up my life. Until I moved here. I had started a new life. I didn't want her input. I had let her know that. This was all very annoying because things had been going well between us. I had set some boundaries and she had mostly respected them. Until today. Time to set some new boundaries. I squared my shoulders and took a deep breath. Ozzy squirmed in my lap.

Aerie pulled her car into the lot between her house and the diner. I got out of the car and set Ozzy on the ground.

Aerie waved me off. "I'll get the produce. Don't worry about it."

"I'll introduce you. She doesn't bite." I took another deep breath and closed the car door.

Ozzy was very excited to meet a new friend. I sighed at her enthusiasm. If I looked toward Aerie, I knew she'd be excited as well. Having a semi-famous sister wasn't all it was cracked up to be. Darla leaned against the passenger door of her Starlight Coupe Studebaker. Dark sunglasses, bouncy curls of raven hair, bright red lipstick.

"There you are." She beamed a dazzling smile in my direction. "The drive was atrocious."

"Your car doesn't have AC," was all I could think to say.

"I had all the windows open the entire time. Mother nature probably hates me for the amount of gas we guzzled on the way down here."

"No one asked you to come visit." I tugged on Ozzy's leash as she made a beeline for Darla. "I didn't ask you to come."

"I called you a million times; you didn't answer. Besides, I've *seen* stuff that's relative to you. You refused to pick up the phone, so I came."

"You could have texted me."

Darla pulled her sunglasses down her nose and stared at me over the top of them. "Really? Nuances in the visions do not come through over texts." She pushed off the car, walked over to me, and wrapped her arms around me. "It's good to see you." Ozzy went ballistic whining and jumping at her ankles. I gave Darla a quick hug in return.

I watched Aerie as she walked my cherries into the diner, wishing I could follow her.

"I suppose you want to stay in the house?"

"Are there any hotels nearby?" Darla reached down and rubbed Ozzy behind the ears.

"You could always drive back home."

"Well, you know I'm not going to do that. I'm actually looking forward to staying with you and seeing what you've done with the house."

I cringed internally. I hadn't done any improvements on the house for the sole reason that after the kitchen burned down it had to be rebuilt with all of the very little money that I had. The construction was somewhat completed, but I didn't have appliances or cabinets yet. I was lucky that Jay helped me rebuild the kitchen. Aerie paid me a decent salary for working at the diner, but it didn't leave much left over for renovation costs.

"You'll have to sleep on the camping cot."

"I've slept on worse. What are you going to do, sleep on the floor?"

How did my sister know I normally slept on the cot? Stupid psychic abilities.

"No. I bought a mattress last week," I said, proudly.

Aerie appeared at my side.

"Darla, this is Aerie, my friend and my boss at the diner."

Darla reached out her hand and Aerie took it.

"Oh," Darla gripped her hand more firmly, "you have a bit of the gift yourself."

Aerie blushed. "I can see auras. But I think that's about it."

"You might be selling yourself short. You're very well grounded. I bet you have remarkable skill."

The flattery caused Aerie to blush. "I *have* been practicing my meditation skills."

"Maybe I can help with that." Darla beamed like a fairy godmother.

"That would be wonderful." Aerie literally grinned ear to ear. A total fan-girl.

Yet another reminder that I was the black sheep of the family with no psychic skills to speak of. Except that I could talk to Arnold, my snarky, entitled cat. And an occasional ghost. But I wasn't about to let Darla in on those little secrets. Plus, I hadn't seen the ghost in a really long time. Maybe she had moved on and out of my house. Which was a good thing, since the old Victorian was becoming a bit of a zoo with Arnold, Ozzy, Taco the parrot, and two giant Koi fish. What would my responsible older sister think of me taking in every stray pet I came across?

I stared at my sister in disbelief that she actually had the nerve to show up here without asking me first. Aerie broke the awkward silence. "Why don't we go up to my kitchen and have some iced tea."

I scooped up Ozzy, turned on my heel toward Aerie's front door, and walked squarely into Jay.

3

———————

"Oh, sorry Mira, I thought you heard me."

I peeled my face off of his broad chest. His close proximity made my insides quiver. When would I get over this stupid crush? He had a girlfriend, after all. My face blazed as I struggled to gain my composure. "Sorry Jay." I turned quickly around to face my sister. "Darla, this is Jay, Aerie's brother. Jay, this is my sister, Darla."

He grinned that miraculous grin and held out a suntanned arm to shake Darla's hand. She looked a little bit flustered, which made me feel incrementally better. For some reason I couldn't wait to tell her that Jay was taken. The notorious Chelsea had his heart, much to the chagrin of both Aerie, me, and pretty much every other woman in Pleasant Pond.

"We were just about to go inside to get something to drink and maybe have some strawberries," Aerie informed Jay.

"I just heard from Dan about the murder. You two were there?"

I watched as Darla perked up. "A murder?"

I scrutinized the look on my sister's face. "That's why you're here, isn't it? You had some crazy vision and it involved me and I wasn't answering the phone and now you're here. That's why, right?"

Jay didn't look surprised when I mentioned my sister's visions. It was annoying how many people knew my famous psychic sister.

"Let's go inside and enjoy some of Aerie's confections." Darla waved for Aerie to lead the way. Everyone followed and I straggled behind.

Eventually Darla would have to spill the truth about why she was here. A moment ago, I just wanted her to go, but now I couldn't wait until we were alone. But first, I needed to hear what Jay knew about the murder victim, and if Dan had shared any details. Murder surpasses overbearing sisters with psychic visions.

Jay held open the door. "Dan told me you bought a desk from the suspect? He gave it to me. It's in the back of my truck." Before I stepped inside Aerie's house, I leaned out and noticed the expertly secured roll-top desk in the flatbed of Jay's pickup truck.

"Thanks, Jay. In all the chaos I forgot about it."

Jay chuckled. "And the fact that Dan was probably shooing you away from the scene. You're like a magnet for all the murders that happen around here."

I could've stomped on Jay's toes at that moment, watching Darla zero in on his exact words. I shook my head; at some point she was going to give me a lecture.

Like a dog with a bone, Darla latched on. "You've been involved in multiple murder investigations?"

I could feel it. Darla was already analyzing the situation.

Jay took the bait. "Dan says the poor guy caught a bullet

straight to the heart. Close range, probably someone he knew."

Aerie shivered. "That's so sad."

I didn't want to discuss the murder in front of my sister. I didn't want her input. But it was more than that. Solving murders had become my thing. My sister already had her crazy thing—her psychic visions and helping the police back in Massachusetts. But I desperately wanted to know what Dan told Jay. "I bet you the murderer was the guy that sold me the desk. He was sweating and nervous and he bugged out of there as soon as he took my forty bucks."

Darla nodded her head thoughtfully. I wanted to scream. I loved my sister, but this was my turf and I didn't want her moving in on my space. I had set boundaries by moving. She was infringing on that. I was trying not to get angrier by the minute.

"Did Dan say anything about who rented that table for the flea market?" I asked Jay. I was convinced that guy was our primary suspect.

"He said he had to check the records. A lot of new people rent tables the week the carnival is here."

Aerie poured tall glasses of lemonade on ice for the four of us. She laid out a plate of cut strawberries. They smelled amazing. Fruit fresh from the farmers market was something I couldn't pass up, even if I was mad at my sister. I bit into the sour-sweet strawberry, and I was right, completely worth it. No matter what Aerie created with these strawberries, it would taste fabulous.

"Has the police department identified the victim yet?" Darla asked.

Jay gulped down his lemonade. "They think he is involved with the carnival, but no name yet."

Darla nodded, closed her eyes, and steepled her fingers.

Both Jay and Aerie held their breath. I disrupted the spectacle immediately. "Darla, I don't think we need a reading right at this moment. I'm sure Detective Lockheart has everything well in hand and doesn't need any assistance from a gifted psychic like yourself." I shot a saccharine smile across the table at her.

She blinked her eyes open and gave me a sour look. "I was only trying to help."

"Sometimes people don't want, or need, your help." I tried to breathe through the irritation tightening my chest, but it was no use. My sister, just being who she was, pushed all my buttons.

Aerie's mouth dropped open and Jay stared at me. I'm sure I lost some brownie points in Jay's book for mouthing off to my sister, but I didn't care. I felt like a nine-year-old again with Darla insisting that I follow her visions.

Aerie stood and took Jay's and her glass to the sink. "I'm sure Dan will take any advice he can get. Goodness knows, Mira, you helped him a few times already."

Ugh. Again, more information my sister didn't need.

"I have to walk Ozzy." I got up and left Aerie and Jay to figure out what to do with my sister.

4

––––––––

Once outside, I took a deep breath. A little space from my sister was just what I needed. Ozzy was less enthused to leave all the people, but a few seconds later she realized we were going for a good walk. I'd take her up to the carnival grounds. It would be about two miles, far enough that I could breathe. I set a brisk pace, which allowed me to stomp out my frustration. Ozzy trotted to keep up. Eventually I slowed down, letting her relieve herself near the trees lining the sidewalk. We passed the recreation center next to the church and continued towards the high school. The tightness in my chest relaxed. I shouldn't hate on Darla so much. And really, I didn't hate my sister. She came to visit to make sure I was okay. I was lucky I had somebody in my life that would do that for me.

At the same time, she was really eager about being helpful with the murder investigation. Probably because solving crimes with the police was a large part of her life back in Massachusetts. I took a deep breath, letting Ozzy sniff everything in sight while I thought this through. Darla could stay, and even help with this murder investigation if she wanted to. Because she would eventually go home, and I would have my life back again. I could give her this gift of being in my life for a short while.

"Come on Ozzy, let's go get everybody and head over to the carnival. We have some investigating to do."

I turned around and headed back.

JAY WAS WAITING, somewhat impatiently, by his truck when I got back. "I just came by to drop off the desk. I really need to get back to the worksite." He drove across the street while I half-heartedly apologized to my sister and led her and Aerie to my house. Jay pulled the desk off his truck and, refusing any help, carried it toward the house. I let Jay in through the porch and he hefted the desk into the living room. I tried not to focus on his biceps too much.

Arnold was overjoyed to see Darla. I swore he loved her more than me sometimes. Probably because she was the first to understand him when he spoke to her and she was all about being the fun Aunt to him. After many cat cuddles and yummy treats, Darla greeted my various pets, as if living in a zoo was totally normal. Taco the macaw whistled and commented on her figure, as wayward birds that grow up in a bar do, and even the two koi fish swam over to say hi face to face.

I grabbed Ozzy a water bowl from the kitchen, making sure my sister was still too occupied with the menagerie to follow me. At some point, I'd have to show her what a complete mess my kitchen was, but I so wasn't in the mood right now.

"Okay. If we're going to solve this murder we better get

started right now. All of us." I'd deal with giving Darla the grand tour of the Victorian later.

The walk was a nice one. I stopped at the ATM at the bank on the way so I could have some carnival fun, shielding my low account balance from my sister. Aerie and Darla got to know each other a bit and I hoped it would make the fan-girling go away. By the time we arrived, it was late afternoon so the carnival hadn't yet turned on their evening lights. My stomach growled at the scent of fried dough and roasting sausages. The Ferris wheel turned above us, and everywhere I looked there were bright colors and laughing people.

Aerie briefly touched my arm to get my attention. "Dan is standing over there. It looks like he's taking a statement." I looked at where she was pointing, to see he was talking to an elderly woman managing the ticket booth. He turned, and...sigh. It was too late; he saw us.

I looked quickly to Darla. "We are not investigating anything. We are just showing you around town. Got it?"

Darla smiled and nodded like she was humoring a child. I didn't have time to go into the hours I spent in a jail cell for getting on Dan's bad side when it came to investigating a case. Worse, he said he had done it for my own good. Everyone could just stop doing things for my own good. I didn't need help running my own life.

Dan strode right up to our little group. "Good evening ladies." He nodded to everyone. "Mira, I hope you're not investigating anything. I do have this under control."

"Nope, Dan, I'm leaving it to you." I stepped back and motioned to Darla. "I'm actually showing my sister around town. Dan, this is my sister Darla."

He smiled broadly as he shook her hand. I watched as the realization dawned. Although it surprised me that Dan would recognize who she was. "You're that psychic, aren't you?"

Darla demurred ever so slightly, grinned, and nodded. "Yes, I am. Darla Damien, nice to meet you."

"Well, Darla Damien, it is an honor to have you in our small town. As you probably know by now there has been a murder today. But I doubt we'll need any type of consulting."

I exhaled a little too loudly. Everyone looked at me.

Dan continued, "I've been completing interviews and I think we're on our way to figuring this one out, but I do hope you have a nice visit here in Pleasant Pond." Dan appeared to be ready to make his exit. But then he stopped. "Mira, can I talk to you for moment? Privately."

This was awkward and out of the ordinary, even for Dan. He walked away from the group and I followed him until he turned around.

"Mira, I was wondering, I know you're busy visiting with your sister but I was hoping maybe you and I could spend some time at the carnival tomorrow evening?"

I froze. I couldn't move a muscle. Had Dan just asked me out on a date? When I started breathing again, I oddly found myself answering, "Sure."

"Great!" This was the most excited I had ever seen Dan in the whole time I've lived here. "Would you like to meet here at 7:30?"

"Okay." I awkwardly turned and walked back to where Aerie and my sister stood.

"What was that all about?" Aerie asked, scanning me up and down.

I had a feeling she was checking out my aura. I wondered what it would tell her. She had been working on that, and I was trying my best to support her with it. After all, I might not want to have other-wordly gifts, but I could support my best friend.

"I'm not sure. But I think Dan just asked me out on a date."

"Yes! It's about time." She celebrated.

Darla leaned forward. "He seems very nice."

"You don't have any visions or vibes that you need to tell me about this guy." It came out sharper than I intended, but I didn't want her to give me any kind of psychic insight on Dan. The less I knew the better. Better to shut it down before it started. I don't even know why I brought it up.

"Come on, I bet we can do some investigating as long as we steer clear of Dan while we're here." I turned everyone around, and we marched the opposite direction.

We slowly made our way through the carnival. Darla cleared her throat. "I feel like we need to talk to the strongman."

I glanced over at the strongman game with its big hammer and equally big strongman. I wondered if Darla was just messing with me or if she wanted to check out the guy for herself. His shirt was off; he obviously did a lot of reps on his pecs and biceps. Neither Aerie nor I disapproved of this recommendation.

As we walked closer, he flexed his muscles for some kids. He made them laugh by alternately flexing his pectoral muscles. The kids giggled and ran away. That's when he spotted us gawking. "Good evening ladies, would any of you like to try your hand at hitting the bell?" He picked up the huge hammer like it weighed nothing. He tossed it from hand to hand, then pointed to me with it. "I bet you could hit the top. Free stuffed animal if you win."

Maybe it was his winning smile, bright dark blue eyes, or those biceps. But I was game. Besides, if I paid to play, maybe we could ask some questions about our suspect. "How much is it for a turn?" I asked.

"Five dollars for three chances."

"That's pretty rich for three chances. I probably won't even get it all the way to the top."

"Guaranteed win! Go ahead and try." His grin melted my reservations. He opened his palm, waiting for my fiver, which I gratefully handed to him, thinking it was worth it to spend a few more minutes at his side. He gently handed me the hammer, handle first.

"Now you want to place your hips just so. Raise the hammer up and put your whole body behind it when you slam it down." His grin was almost as distracting as his biceps. I took a deep breath, planted my feet, tensed the ab muscles I had been toning in Aerie's yoga class, swung back the hammer, and slammed it forward.

The hammer connected with the lever and popped the weight up only halfway. Lights lit up its trail and slowly went dark as the weight fell back down.

"Good try. You got two more chances."

"I let the hammer drop to my side. I looked to Aerie and Darla. "Can I give my chances to my friends?"

"Um, sure. Why not?" He graciously waved his arm. I handed the hammer to Aerie. She planted her feet, squared her legs and hit that hammer with all her might. Admittedly she was in better shape than me. I was surprised when it didn't go quite as high as mine. She laughed and handed it to Darla for a try.

"Sure." Darla shrugged. "I haven't done one of these in ages. I think the last time was when we were ten or eleven at that carnival in Maine. Do you remember, Mira?"

"Nope." I did not want to go down memory lane with Darla right at this moment. She swung and hit the weight, which went up just a few notches and came back down. "Oh, well." Darla handed the hammer back to Mr. Adonis.

"That means you, young lady, are the winner of the prize."

"But none of us hit the bell," I protested.

"I did say that everyone's a winner!"

He pulled down three small stuffed dogs and gave them to us, handing the last to me. "Thanks." I took the dog from his big strong hand. "Can I ask you something?"

"Sure."

"Did you hear about the murder this afternoon?"

He obviously wasn't expecting that as a question. He cleared his throat a couple of times. "Yeah. Poor guy." He shook his head in sympathy.

"Did you know him?"

"No." He answered a little too quickly. "No, I didn't know the guy."

"Do you know anybody that works at the flea market?"

"A couple of the carnies manage tables each time we come to town. It helps them with their wages. We pay well, but every little bit counts, right?"

"Do you know anybody that wears a blue hat with a dolphin on it?"

He shifted from foot to foot. "No. There is one guy who always wears a baseball hat. I've seen him around here a couple times. Think his name is Ray. But I don't know the guy."

A clue. I reached out my hand and gave him a bright smile. "Thank you very much for your time Mr...."

"Palmer. But you call me Tony. It was nice meeting you."

"My name is Mira. Thanks for the dog." I awkwardly held up the stuffed toy. "Have a good night." I turned to

Aerie and Darla. "I think we should cut our losses before Dan finds us."

Aerie agreed. She knew Dan better than anybody.

Darla gave me that look. That look that told me I was about to do something wrong.

"What?" I asked.

"Nothing. Just be careful." Darla closed and opened her eyes, and took a breath. "I feel like we got the information that we were supposed to get. And I am more than a little bit hungry."

Now the awkwardness would really begin. I'd have to explain to my sister why I did not have a working, functional kitchen. I'd have to fess up to the fire a month ago. I thought I'd leave out the part about it being a murder scene the day I moved in, however.

Luckily Aerie, always the best friend, jumped to my aid. "We can open up the diner real quick and have a proper dinner."

"I'll cook." I heartily agreed.

Darla looked slightly surprised. In a small way I was excited to share my new skill set. I only hoped she'd like my cooking.

WE MEANDERED DOWN the field and away from the carnival. My head spun with the idea of going on a date with Dan. Was I crazy? The man had put me in jail once. Granted he felt he was protecting me at the time, but jail? I must be crazy. Something about him made me curious. He was normal. Relatively. I mean he wasn't like any of the crazies I dated before, the relationships that crashed and burned dramatically, every single time. I was making a life change here in Pleasant Pond. Maybe this could be the start of a normal relationship. Oh, who was I kidding, it was just a date. One date.

"What?" Both Aerie and Darla were staring at me.

"Mira's kitchen burned down a few months ago," Aerie said. Obviously, I'd missed something. Probably Darla asking why we weren't eating at my place. "She's a great cook at the diner."

"I never knew you had an affinity for cooking, Mira." She walked between Aerie and I, her glossy black curls highlighted by the evening sun. "You always hated that job at the Italian restaurant."

I grunted. "It's because the maître d' always hit on me. He was a real sleaze ball."

Darla nodded knowingly. "Of all the auras, his was a mess. You should have seen it, Aerie. You would have known in a heartbeat that he had issues."

Ugh, another one of Darla's favorite past times, stressing all the ways she's a psychic and I am not. I'm the ungifted one. I quickened my pace as we got closer to the diner, pulled out my keys, and unlocked the door. I flipped on the lights. The glow of the black checked floor and the blue vinyl booths calmed my nerves. This place soothed my soul.

I went straight back to the kitchen and flipped on the fryer. It would take a bit of time for it to heat up but after smelling all the fried food at the carnival I craved something crispy. I wasn't very hungry, but I could show off the one skill I did have, slinging hash, frying up decent diner meals.

I could hear Aerie out front with her chipper voice welcoming Darla to her diner, asking her to have a seat and offering a menu. After months of cooking here I could pretty much throw anything together off the menu with ease. Except maybe the soup, which took some planning.

Currently we'd stopped serving soup to focus on ice cream. We already had quite a few ice cream flavors in the freezer. Even so, I couldn't wait to experiment with those fresh cherries.

I turned on the grill and walked out front to pretend to have civil conversation with my sister, for Aerie's sake. It was still a little obvious that she was fan-girling.

"Everything is heating up. You guys just let me know what you want and I can cook it for you." I slid into the booth next to Aerie.

Darla scanned the menu with a grin on her face. "Aerie, you have a great menu. Everything sounds wonderful. I especially like your vegan options." She ran a finger down the right side of the menu where Aerie had highlighted her vegan options for the diner. "Can I get the mushroom slider with vegan cheese?" She lowered the menu slightly so her eyes peeked over the top. She directed her question at me, and for the first time I noticed she had eyelash extensions, like her big green eyes needed anything more to call attention to them.

"Sure," I said. "How do you want the mushroom, medium rare?"

"Always the jokester." Darla shook her head and put down the menu.

On that note, I disappeared back into the kitchen.

We had a few trays of large portobello mushrooms that we used as a meat substitute. When the mushrooms were past their prime, I made soup with them. They didn't have to look pretty if they were in a cream-based soup. They also worked well in the chicken and rice casserole we recently added to the menu. Mrs. Orsa was kind enough to share her family recipe.

I started the mushroom burgers. The dollop of plant-based butter sizzled on the grill. I grabbed the top and bottom of the buns, slid them through the butter and then set them on the warming section of the grill. I wanted them warm but not toasted. Next, I put two large portobello mushroom tops onto the hot grill and sprinkled them with our proprietary seasoned salt. While they heated up, I went into the freezer and grabbed a bag of fries, dumped a good amount into the fryer basket, and dropped it into the hot oil. After a few minutes I flipped the mushrooms and placed slices of the vegan cheese on both. I put a lid over the mushrooms, poured a few tablespoons of water, on the grill and closed the lid. The steam from the water helped to melt the cheese.

Now that the cheese had melted, I grabbed the spatula, slid both mushroom burgers onto their buns, and plated them.

When the timer went off on the fryer, I lifted the basket, shook out the fries, and added a dash of the seasoned salt. I took a deep breath, grabbed the plates and headed into the dining room.

5

I placed the heavy white plates on the Formica tabletop. "Ooh, this looks good." Darla grinned at me. "I'm excited to try your cooking."

"Well, it won't poison you. That was last month." I snickered.

Darla raised an eyebrow with a mouthful of mushroom. Her chewing slowed. She put a hand to her mouth. "What?"

Aerie swallowed her bite. "Last month Mira was accused of poisoning one of our patrons. Which, of course, was a complete lie and fabrication, and we proved it by finding the actual killer."

I shrugged. "It was a group effort." I remembered how snarky-Chelsea, Jay's girlfriend, and Aerie had managed things while I, no thanks to Dan, was incapacitated in a jail cell. Obviously, I had issues with this. Why had I agreed to go on a date with him? I shook my head then stuffed my mouth full of french fries.

Darla appeared to be enjoying her mushroom burger. "This cheese is really good."

"Thanks. We buy direct from the company that makes it.

I sampled all of their cheeses. This one was my favorite." Aerie was proud of her business.

"So, how do you plan on working this case?" Darla asked Aerie, but her eyes slowly gazed in my direction. Her question was really geared toward me. She was testing the waters to see if I had taken up her calling to help solve crimes.

Aerie leaned forward. "After learning that the guy in the blue baseball cap might be named Ray, we can go on that and try to find out who else knows him. Won't we, Mira?" Aerie loved a good mystery.

"I dunno. I promised Dan I wouldn't look into it."

"Really?" Aerie squeaked, almost spitting out her fries.

Darla shifted in her seat. "Oh, come on, this will be fun. I could help."

"Dan doesn't like to receive help when it comes to dealing with crime in Pleasant Pond. If you want to go ahead and try to help him, you're more than welcome." I wanted to prove to Darla that I had just as good of a skill set as she did when it came to solving crime, but I had an inkling if Dan caught me meddling again, our date would be off. And I really wanted something normal, even if it was a stupid date. What I didn't want was Darla to become the shining star within my group of friends. I wanted a life where I wasn't overshadowed by my famous sister.

"Oh, Mira, it'll be fun. Darla can use her psychic skills and you and I can work together. We already have a great clue with this Ray guy, and with Darla's help, I bet we'll catch the killer before Dan does."

"I really don't care about finding this guy. Or about solving the mystery." I completely and totally lied.

"Why not? We do it all the time." Aerie squinted at me.

I stood. "I don't want to do it this time." What I didn't

want to do was openly compete with my sister to solve this murder. I stood up and walked out the front door. I needed to walk off the stress of being around my sister; the competitiveness between the two of us is just too much. I needed to walk it off. Again.

I headed in the direction of the general store. If they asked, I'd just say I needed a stick of gum. Why did my sister always make me feel so inferior?

I should relax. She was only being friendly and trying to help. I took a deep breath. Yes, I would walk to the store and get myself a pack of gum and then just go back and apologize. See, I was being the bigger person. Someone that Dan wouldn't mind dating.

About a hundred yards from the general store, I watched a man come out and cross the street away from me. There was something oddly familiar about his walk. When it hit me, I shook my head. "No. It couldn't be." I must be having past relationship PTSD. There was no way that could be Alex. I needed my eyes checked; maybe I need glasses. Because if Alex Williams was in town, my life was in the crapper.

I didn't bother going to the store. I turned right around and went back to the diner. When I got there, I flung open the door. "I think I just saw Alex." Both Darla and Aerie were in the process of clearing their dishes and heading toward the kitchen. Aerie turned, looking confused. "Who's that?"

Darla shook her head. "Nobody you want to know. Are you sure it's him?"

"He didn't follow you here?"

Darla looked surprised. "Why would Alex follow me?"

"To get to me."

"Why? He already took all your money."

"How else could he be here? How would he know I live here? *You* barely know where I live."

"I have no idea why he's here."

"What, is your psychic mumbo-jumbo on the fritz? Don't you have some *feeling* about it, why would he be here? My life was a mess because of him. I finally got it back on track, and out of the blue he shows up?"

"My visions have been disastrous lately so it's just as big a mystery to me as it is to you." Darla turned and went into the kitchen.

Aerie followed, and I could hear them washing the dishes. I walked over to the booth, sat down heavily and stared at my plate of cold fries, stuffing a few in my mouth. I closed my eyes. First Darla showed up, then Dan asked me out, and now Alex is in town? That's not even counting the dead body I found today. This was turning out to be one heck of a week.

6

———

After we cleaned and closed the diner, Aerie went home and Darla and I got in her Studebaker so she could park it in front of my house. The scent of the car triggered memories of childhood and home and all the great times Darla and I had. Fun times we had before things went downhill. When the psychic stuff became a business and things fell apart. I pushed it out of my mind. This car was a beauty and I was glad to see it again.

"I can't believe you drove her all the way down here." I ran my fingers over the metal V8 symbol in the center of the dash.

"I contemplated getting a rental, but I knew you'd like to see her as much, if not more, than seeing me."

I grinned. "Thanks. Can we drive around the block?"

"Sure." She put the Starlight in gear, and we drove toward the general store.

"Is this where you saw Alex?"

"Ugh, I don't even like hearing his name."

"If you had listened to me..."

"Let's not rehash that all over again."

"At least this time you won't fall for his faux charm."

"That's for sure," I said under my breath.

"How are you doing here?"

"Is that why you came? To find out how I was doing?"

Her shoulders tightened and I could tell she was waffling over what to say. "That's part of it. It looks like you have a good work situation at the diner. That burger you made was great."

"Thanks. I'm still learning. Aerie needed the help and I need the cash."

"Her brother is rebuilding the kitchen?" she asked haltingly.

"He's involved with someone. Don't get your hopes up."

"He's involved with someone who's a bit controlling." She shrugged. "Hey, you never know, things could change." She grinned.

"Still amazes me how you pick up on that stuff." And it did. Darla hadn't met Chelsea and yet she knew she was controlling. I had to respect how spot-on her psychic knowledge could be.

"I'd say it's still a surprise to me too, except, at this point I've just accepted that this is who I am." She slowed the car as we approached the house. "We can park right behind Babs here."

"I didn't think you knew her name."

"You always name cars. You've had this one forever."

"She still runs, most of the time. Come on, let's get your stuff inside. You'd probably be more comfortable in a B&B or something. This house isn't quite cozy yet."

I unlocked the door and stepped inside. Immediately I was given the third degree by Arnold my loving but snarky long-haired black cat.

Where have you been? It's been all day. I haven't had a single treat in six hours!

Regardless of his displeasure with me he rubbed his face against my shin. And that's when he noticed Darla.

Darla! You're forgiven.

Darla bent over and scooped up Arnold. "Hey buddy. I missed you." She rubbed the spot between his ears that I knew he absolutely loved. His purr could be heard for miles.

Ozzy jumped around for attention.

"I didn't get a chance to ask you before: When did you get this little terrier? She's adorable." Darla watched as Ozzy paced and jumped, happy to see us.

"Just after I moved here, the original cook at the diner had to leave town and couldn't take her with him."

"How does Arnold feel about this?" She stroked his head and neck.

She is tolerable.

I was not about to let Darla in on the secret that I could hear Arnold's actual thoughts. I didn't want to start comparing skill sets. It would just make me feel like crap.

"I dunno. Ask him?" I challenged her.

She put Arnold down and he flopped on his back with his furry belly in the air and Darla smoothed his fur. "I think he tolerates her."

I shook my head; he rarely let me rub his belly. Picky cat.

"Love on him all you want; he obviously misses you." I took her suitcase and decided to put it in the "guest" room. I was grateful it was summer and I didn't have to worry about heating the upstairs. That would be a problem I'd have to solve later.

"Wait. I'll come with you. I'd love to have the grand tour."

I watched as Arnold followed reverently behind her.

"Well, we're in the dining room. Over there is the place that will be the kitchen. I pointed to the drywalled space bereft of countertops, cabinets, or appliances. Before she could look at it any closer, I walked down the hallway toward the living room.

"Over here is the living room." I motioned to the open room to the left. The room was large, and the back door and wraparound porch were off this room and the family room next to it. For all the space, the only items here were the secondhand couch and recliner, and of course, the desk.

"Is this the desk you purchased from the suspected murderer?"

"Yes." The rolltop desk still had a golden shine to it that didn't scream *murderous owner* on it at all.

Darla walked to it and ran her fingers along the top. I knew what she was doing. She was attempting to pick up any kinds of vibrations from it. Any clues. They usually appeared to her like quick photographs in her mind. That's how she explained it to me anyway. Not being psychic, I wouldn't know.

I asked her, "Do you feel anything?"

"It's obviously connected to the situation. I don't feel anything negative or intense about it."

"That's not entirely helpful."

She shot me a frustrated look I wasn't used to seeing from her. "I thought you didn't want to look into the murder?"

"You're right. I don't," I said with finality. "Let me show you upstairs."

We climbed the steep narrow stairway to the top. I glanced back, and, yes, Arnold was following us.

I pointed in the direction of the bathroom, showed her

which bedroom was mine and walked further down the hallway to the guest room where she would be staying.

"Oh." She tried to hide her surprise but there was no denying it.

"You were expecting something a little more, furnished?"

"Well, yeah."

"I am not the psychic sister who makes ten grand at each showing. Just a diner chef attempting to save up for the stupid kitchen refurbish."

We stood and stared at the army cot in the middle of the room, recently moved over from my room when I finally bought a real mattress to sleep on. That was it. No nightstand, no mattress, no photos hanging on the wall.

"If you had let me know you were coming, I could've made it look a little more appealing."

"Oh, no, it's fine. It'll be fine," she lied through her teeth.

"There is a bed-and-breakfast in town. I can look up the number."

"No. I want to stay with you. Even if it's on the cot," she sincerely said. "Oh, do you have a clawfoot tub in the bathroom?"

"Actually yes. You want to see it?"

"Of course. Lead the way." The two of us, three of us if Arnold was included, and he always wanted to be included where Darla was involved, made our way down the hall to the bathroom.

Arnold rumbled low in his throat. *Oh, hello Clara.*

Clara passed through me like an ice storm, raising all the hairs in the back of my neck. I shivered. And then I heard my sister. "Oh." Like she had sat on a tack. "Cold spot, ah, female 1800's. You have someone here. Did you know that?"

"That's just Clara." I slapped my hand over my mouth. Regret caused my face to burn.

"Ha, I knew it. I knew you had the gift!"

"I am not psychic. We're not talking about it." I spent too much time cultivating the notion that I was not like my sister. I was not psychic. I was comfortable in my denial and I planned to stay that way. I turned around and walked back downstairs. If she wanted to find out if we had a clawfoot tub she could go into the bathroom herself. I refused to be anywhere around the idea that I was psychic.

"Then how do you know her name is Clara?" she shouted down to me.

Halfway down the stairs I shouted back, "Because she told Arnold."

"So, you can understand Arnold, too?"

I stopped in the middle of the staircase and turned around to look at her. "You can hear him?"

Of course she can hear me, that's why I love her so much.

"Have you talked to Clara through Arnold?"

"No. But we've come to a mutual agreement to share the house."

Darla raised her eyebrow. "The only reason she would still be in this plane is if she needs something."

"Oh really?"

"Yes. Would you like me to ask her for you?"

"No. No, not really."

Darla gave me a look that I knew meant she would ask Clara anyway. I turned around and marched down the rest of the stairs.

We didn't talk much the rest of the night. Darla unpacked her suitcase and got ready for bed and shut her door.

I was about ready to collapse. I got into bed thinking that

maybe Clara did need something. But I couldn't wonder about that now. My stomach was tied in knots at the thought of going on a first date with Dan tomorrow. I just wanted to make sure I didn't do or say anything stupid. But that wasn't the only thing making me anxious. Something about seeing Alex again set off every nerve in my body. What could he be doing in the middle of Pennsylvania? This wasn't exactly a big hub of the Northeast. He had already stolen all my money and whatever pride I actually had. What else was there? Maybe, he wanted to say he was sorry? But that seemed highly unlikely. Remorse was not something that Alex ever showed while we dated. What could he possibly want?

7

———

I woke up to the sound of Arnold's meow. He was better than any alarm clock and it was early enough that I could attend Aerie's yoga class before we opened the diner. After donning my yoga leggings and yoga top, I headed down the hall. I knocked lightly on Darla's door.

"Come in." She sounded groggy.

"Hey, I'm heading out to a yoga class and then I'm going to open the diner. I'll be there until 2:45."

"I have some remote readings scheduled for today." She sat up on her elbows. "I'll come by for breakfast."

"Sure." I cringed. I remember how uncomfortable the cot was. She probably hadn't slept very well. "You can sleep in my bed for the rest of the morning if you want."

"No, it's okay. I should get up anyway. Thanks, though." She swung her legs off the cot and stretched. "I'll see you at the diner later?" She arched her back and ran a hand through her curls.

"See you there." I pulled her door gently closed and headed downstairs to feed Arnold and Ozzy. I had to remember to take Ozzy for a brief walk.

Arnold sat at the base of the stairs. *Is Darla staying forever?*

"No, Arnold, she's not staying forever. Just a couple days, maybe."

He moped. Or as close as a cat could mope. "I'm sure she will give you lots of pats before she leaves. Come on, I'll get you some kitty treats to cheer you up."

Arnold followed with Ozzy close at my ankles all the way into the kitchen. I placed a big handful of treats on the floor for Arnold. Ozzy's primary concern was breakfast. After Ozzy finished her breakfast, I took her for a quick walk in front of the house. Then headed to yoga. Aerie and I had a plan where she'd start class a bit earlier, and then I'd duck out before she finished so I could open the diner. By the time I got to the diner I had to rush in to set everything up. Moments later, Mrs. Orsa appeared, ready for her breakfast.

"Tea and a muffin?" I asked her.

"Yes, thank you, Mira. Is it the pineapple coconut ones? Those were excellent yesterday."

"Yes, we still have a few left." Those muffins actually sold out fast, but Mrs. Orsa rescued me from a murderer when I first came to town, so I had a soft spot for her and had held back one of the delectable delights for her.

I walked into the kitchen to retrieve the muffin from the refrigerator. I ran my hands over the stash of cherries and strawberries we had purchased yesterday. I secretly hoped the breakfast rush would be slow so I could work on the cherry almond ice cream I had planned.

The bell over the door rang and Aerie greeted Mrs. Orsa. I placed the pineapple coconut muffin with its thin layer of whipped cream cheese icing on a small plate and carried it out to the dining room.

Aerie was pouring Mrs. Orsa hot water for her morning tea.

"Hey, Aerie, thanks for bringing in the fruit we bought yesterday."

"I'm looking forward to working on the strawberry parfait today. I'm going to try to make coconut whipped cream to layer with the strawberries."

"That sounds fabulous. If you need help just let me know." The idea of strawberries and coconut cream made my mouth water. I placed the plate in front of Mrs. Orsa.

"Thank you, dear." Mrs. Orsa grinned up at me.

"You're welcome, Mrs. Orsa. You let me know if you need anything."

She smiled and nodded and dug into her muffin.

Aerie and I walked back toward the counter.

"Will your sister be joining us this morning?"

"Yes, but first she has some remote readings that she has to do." When Aerie gave me a confused look, I explained, "She meets with her clients over a video chat and advises them that way."

I could tell that Aerie was really interested and wanted to ask more questions, but she knew better than to ask me about it. She could wait until Darla showed up to find out more.

"Anything she wants is on the house."

"That's fine, Aerie. Thanks." I had to grin. I knew she was still a fan-girl of Darla. And that was okay. I was getting used to it.

Soon we had our regular fill of customers for the early morning rush. Once the initial rush subsided, I figured this was my chance. "Aerie, if it's okay, I'm going to work on the cherry syrup for the ice cream.

"Sounds good. I'm almost done cleaning out here."

"Do you need any help?"

"No. Get working on that cherry ice cream. I'm hungry for it."

"I'm going to create a cashew milk base, too." It was always fun to see how the different flavors of the nut milks melded with the fruit.

I took the cherries out of the refrigerator and placed them on the counter, and the slow realization hit, I was going to have to pit every single one of those cherries. All five pounds of them. "Um, hey, Aerie?" I shouted into the dining room. "Do you have a cherry pitter?"

I heard her stifle a giggle. "Yes. It's on the top shelf of the pantry."

Oh, good. "Thanks!"

Aerie walked into the kitchen carrying the container of dirty dishes. "The cherry-pitter is over there." She nodded her head toward the pantry shelves. On the top shelf sat a small clear box with a white top.

I picked it up. "This thing?" I had never seen anything like it before. I had thought a handheld single cherry-pitter was the only option. This looked like you dumped a handful into it and one would drop into an area where you could use the plunger to push the pit into the container. The newly pitted cherry would fall out the back. "This looks interesting."

"I'm not a huge fan of pitting cherries." Aerie placed the dishes on the counter and began to rinse them off. "But after you get the hang of it, it can be kind of meditative."

"I'll take your word for it." I pulled the cherry pitter device off the shelf and carried it over to the sink for a quick rinse.

I grabbed the largest colander we had, placed it in the

sink, and dumped in the cherries. After washing the cherries, I was ready to go.

"You probably want to sit on the stool or something," Aerie suggested.

"Good idea." We had a tall step stool that we used to reach things at the top of the shelves. But it could also be used as somewhere to sit. This looked like a task that was going to take a while. I dropped six or seven cherries into the opening at the top and watched as a single cherry fell into the slot. I pushed the plunger and cherry juice sprayed in the inside of the little box and the pit dropped out. I released the plunger and the cherry fell onto the counter. "Oops. I need a bowl."

I picked up the cherry and popped it into my mouth. I washed my hands and got another bowl to place under the slot for the cherries.

About thirty cherries in, I realized two things. Contrary to common thought about this device shielding you from all of the cherry juice, it did not, and cherry juice stains everything, including your hands. Still, the idea of making a cherry almond ice cream was worth the trouble. After almost an hour of emptying the container like a hundred times, I had the cherries pitted.

Now to make a type of cherry syrup to add to the different ice cream bases.

I measured out the cherries and placed them in a large pot. After adding the right amount of sugar, I turned the burner on low. The lunch rush would start soon. I didn't want to put the heat up and have to worry about the cherries burning. I swirled a long handled wooden spoon through the mixture. I could smell the sour sweet scent of the cherries as they warmed.

"Mira." Aerie swung around the corner. "Dan is here.

He'd like to ask us both some questions about what we saw yesterday."

"Sure. This is under control." I glanced at the pot and headed into the dining room. I tried not to think about the fact I had told him we could go out on a date.

Dan stood at the front of the counter with his flip notepad and pen at the ready.

I wiped my hands on the dishtowel. "You sure you don't want lunch first, before it gets busy?" Dan was a fan of my hamburgers and fries, but lately he had been opting for the healthier vegan options that Aerie and I had added to the menu. "Falafel with tzatziki?" Last week we had purchased cucumbers from Mr. Miller's vegetable gardens.

"Maybe. But not yet." He was cute when he was ruffled. "I need to ask both of you a few more questions about what happened yesterday." Dan was always so good about not blurting out the words murder and body or any other gory details while he was in the diner. Which Aerie and I both appreciated.

"Sure. What else do you need to know?" Aerie asked.

"Well, it appears that the gentleman who sold you the desk was not Mr. Miller's cousin. And we are still trying to ascertain who he might be. You're sure he had a blue cap on when you saw him?"

"He definitely had on a blue hat."

"And you said he was behaving in a way that seemed nervous?"

"He sold me a desk that was worth three times the amount. He pocketed the money I gave him and then he ran off."

"Can you describe exactly what he looked like?"

I gave him a description—the guy was just normal-looking. Brown hair, regular build, neither thin nor heavy. Totally non-descript but I did the best I could.

Dan wrote in his notebook, then closed and pocketed it. He took a deep breath. "I would really enjoy a falafel if you have time."

"Coming right up." I hopped back into the kitchen, grabbed the container of falafel batter out of the fridge and prepared to make Dan's current favorite lunch. Within minutes the lunch rush began. We were busy once more. I didn't even have time to go and make sure Dan enjoyed his falafel. I reminded myself to check the cherry jam that was slowly simmering on stove. It smelled fabulous. I couldn't wait to taste the ice cream it would make. Halfway through lunch, I turned off the burner to let it cool down. I'd have to chill it until I was ready to make the ice cream base. By how intense the lunch had started I wasn't sure when that would be.

"Hey, Mira, Dan had to go, but he said he'll see you tonight." She grinned like crazy. "You better give me all the details."

"You're being silly; it's just a date."

"But you like Dan, right?"

"Sometimes he makes me crazy."

"Like all true romances." She swooned.

"Like all failed romances." All of mine, at least.

"Oh, don't start. You guys would look really cute together. And then you and I could go on double dates."

"I am not doing karaoke at Sam's ever again. That did not end well last time."

The bell sounded on the door. Aerie turned to head back into the dining room. "Tonight will be fun. And I still want the details. You will call me, right?"

"Of course." I would probably need moral support.

Aerie ducked back out to the dining room to attend to the lunch customers. But she came right back. "Someone is asking for you out front." She gave me a questioning glance.

"Someone?"

Aerie knew everyone in town and although the occasional Pennsylvania Grand Canyon tourist got lost and ended up here, Aerie knew everyone who entered the diner.

"Okay." Confused and curious, I set some items on a lower temperature at the grill and headed out to see who would actually ask to see me. Which reminded me...Darla hadn't shown up yet for her breakfast, and it was past lunchtime.

The moment I turned the corner, I regretted leaving the kitchen.

My detestable ex-boyfriend, who stole all my cash six months ago, was sitting at the counter like he was waiting for a dentist appointment.

As soon as he saw me though he painted on his goofy grin and turned to face me. "Mira! I heard from one of my fellow carnies you worked here."

After the initial shock wore off, I was quick to set the facts straight. "Alex, this is my place of business. I highly recommend you leave. Quickly. Before I call the cops on your sorry, thieving chinos."

"Thieving?" he questioned, and then I could tell he thought better of what he was about to say. "No, you're right. I shouldn't have left things that way with you, Mira."

"No kidding." Was he seriously saying he was sorry? What a scam artist. I needed to kick his sorry but cute rear to the curb. "Alex, you really..."

"I know, I really need to say I'm sorry." He leaned forward and before I knew it, he held my hand. "I want to make it up to you. Let me take you to dinner tonight."

I yanked my hand out of his spidery fingers. "No. Alex. We're over. And thanks to you, I'm still trying to climb out of debt. I don't have any more money for you to steal from me."

"Just tonight, just one date? I'll come over and bring a bottle of wine. Like the old days."

"The old days. Like when you lied, cheated, and stole my life savings?" For a second, he looked hurt, and I was glad. "Besides, I have a date tonight."

"You do?" He sounded surprised.

"Don't say it like it's a shock!"

He painted that grin on his face. "Fine, be that way Mir, but I'll tell you, I'll wait for you. Maybe tomorrow?"

"Get out before I throw something at your head." I lifted the sugar shaker and hefted it dangerously.

"I'll come back tomorrow."

I raised the sugar shaker higher. He cut the grin short and turned tail.

"Don't come back at all," I shouted at his retreating form.

Mr. Meyer from the bank, watched Alex leave and went back to his meal. Aerie offered to refill his coffee.

I stormed my way into the kitchen.

IT WASN'T long after that Darla came in for lunch. I heard her greet Aerie when she entered the diner. She climbed onto one of the stools at the counter and Aerie offered her some ice water.

"Sorry I'm late, I had a couple readings that ran over. And then I had to make changes to my online class because it wasn't uploading to my website properly. It was a mess."

"We're glad you're here. Anything you want for lunch is

on the house," Aerie said in her chipper, buoyant voice as she handed Darla the menu.

"Thanks."

I walked out from the kitchen. "I can make you falafel. We have some extra batter in the back."

"You wouldn't mind?"

"Not at all. I can cook more than just burgers."

"You showed that to me yesterday. I believe you."

"Okay, then. This is just so I can flaunt it."

"Have at it. I'm hungry for falafel."

"We have fresh tzatziki as well. Just made it yesterday."

I put together Darla's falafel platter with fresh tomatoes, onions, and cucumber and grilled pita bread. I wedged a small sauce dish on the side of the plate and added a good heaping spoonful of the tzatziki sauce. The dill and garlic scent made my mouth water as I put the creamy cucumber sauce in the dish.

We finished the lunch rush soon after that. I came out to see how Darla was doing with her meal. "Mira, seriously this is like the best falafel I've had in a long time."

I shrugged absently, but I secretly loved the recognition. "Aerie and I make sure the menu is as fresh as possible."

"It shows." Darla lifted the fork to her mouth and licked the last of the sauce. She gave me a sly smile. "Could you make this for me again, tomorrow?"

"Sure. What are sisters for?" I smiled too happily, but I couldn't help myself.

Aerie and I started our regular closing duties. Darla even walked her dish back into the kitchen.

After cleaning and getting a little bit too much ribbing about my date with Dan the detective, the three of us locked up the diner. Darla and I were ready to go back to the house. I needed a shower and a change of clothes, and Darla wanted to check to make sure her online class was loading properly for her students.

Ozzy also needed a nice long walk. When we got to the front door, it was unlocked and slightly ajar. Carefully, I pushed the door open. I turned quickly to Darla and put my finger to my mouth telling her to stay quiet. She violently shook her head, grabbed my arm, and pulled out her phone, I assumed to call the police.

For the second time in a few months, I was baffled as to why anyone would break into my place. I owned absolutely nothing of value. I shook off my sister's protective hold on my arm, tiptoed inside, and scanned the dining room. Nobody. I glanced into the kitchen and with its white walls and lack of anything else. No one was in there.

Nervously, I made my way down the hallway toward the living room when I heard hissing and growls from a very irate cat. Arnold. I rushed into the living room to see a blue baseball-capped man dash out the back door onto the porch. I raced across the room following him, not quite sure what I would do if I caught him. Sit on him until someone showed up? But he was faster than me. I caught a glimpse of him as he ran off the porch. Yep, blue baseball cap, same guy that sold me the desk. I walked back into the living room.

Arnold stood on top of the desk, haunches raised, tail straight and poofed out to its maximum height. With his black fur standing on end, he looked like the biggest electrified puffball. "What was that all about?"

Obviously, I got rid of the cat burglar for you. You're welcome.

"That's the guy that sold me the desk. Did he want it back? What happened?"

I decided the sun in the living room was getting a bit too hot for me, so I came over here and climbed inside the drawer.

I knew better than to ask him to explain his cat proclivity

for curling up inside of boxes and drawers. It was just a Thing.

I had pulled this drawer open and was sitting in it because it was so cozy. Then this smelly human appeared. Instead of petting me, he tried to get me out of my cozy drawer. Forget that. It was the most comfortable spot I've had in days. I had to leave claw marks. That guy will be sore for a while.

"I'm sure." I moved closer to the drawer and noticed Arnold's fluffy backside rested on something.

"Were you sitting on this piece of paper?"

Yes. Of course, I was. Paper, blankets, all that stuff insulates, it's quite wonderful to rest one's body on.

I shook my head. Nope, I would never understand cats.

I heard Darla's footsteps come down the hallway. "Are you okay?"

"Arnold scared them off. Didn't you, buddy?" I rubbed under his neck.

"I called the police. They should be here soon."

"Great. It'll probably be Dan." I shook my head. I really didn't want him to see me all greasy and hot and sweaty from working at the diner all morning. I laughed to myself. Not too long ago, I wouldn't have cared how Dan Lockheart saw me. Now that he was looking at me like a woman instead of the diner chef who kept getting tangled up in his investigations, I felt a bit self-conscious.

There was one thing I wanted to do before he got here. I took the piece of paper from the drawer and pulled out my phone from my back pocket. I took five or six photos quickly and stuffed my phone into my pocket.

When Dan arrived, I was surprised to realize his primary concern was my safety. Had he always been this way? It made me feel warm, and I found it charming. I gave him the rundown of everything that I witnessed, excluding some of the details given to me by Arnold. I showed him the piece of paper. "I think the guy was after this." He took the paper from me looked it over. I already knew it was some kind of cipher. A coded message of some sort.

"I'm going to take this in as evidence. I won't confiscate your desk, but I would like to look it over closely."

"Sure, Dan, whatever."

"We've been able to identify the murder victim, a Joel Bauer, who worked for the folks at the carnival."

I watched as he inspected the desk and took some quick photos with his phone. Dan usually wouldn't share details on the investigations with me, not without prompting anyway. New world, I guess. I picked up Arnold and stroked his back, asking him in my mind if he was okay too.

No bruises?

I'm in desperate need of kitty treats.

Of course, you are.

"Come on, Arnold, I'll get you some treats. Dan, if you'll excuse us?"

"Sure. I'll only be a couple more minutes." He had crawled under the desk and was looking at the underside.

I carried Arnold into the kitchen. Now that it had four walls and a ceiling, I could actually store things in here. I had a little pantry cabinet where I kept the cat food and, of course, the cat treats. I gave Arnold a full handful of the obviously tasty squares. He deserved them.

I walked back into the living room. Darla and Dan were speaking in low whispers. Something about "watching over her for her own good," and Dan agreeing. Who were they discussing? Me? Suddenly I was furious. Where did Darla get off telling Dan to watch over me? And he agreed!?

They were not expecting me. I could tell by the guilty way they looked up when I walked in.

"What's this deal about watching over me? I'm not some child. I'm an adult who can live my own life however I want." I jabbed my finger at Darla. "You come back into my life and try to run it. No. No more." Fuming, I paced back and forth. "Dan, you can forget about the date."

Sheepishly, he gathered up the paper, closed the drawers to the desk and quickly walked around me out of the room. I heard the front door close.

Darla looked like she was about to burst into tears, or yell at me, or both. Before she could say anything, I cut her off. "You can't come here and run my life anymore. That's why I moved."

"I know, but I have this premonition you're in trouble. Something about a number of men lying to you..."

"Lying to me? Do you think that's worse than trying to control my life? Worse than coming into my new life and trying to talk my possible boyfriend-something-or-other into watching over me? This is wrong on so many levels."

I stormed out of the room. "Come on, Ozzy. It's time for your walk." It sounded a little more like a yell than I wanted, but Ozzy didn't appear to mind. She bounced up and down, clearly excited for another walk. I latched her leash to her collar. Arnold paced. He had heard our fight. I wondered whose side he was on.

I'm on yours. He sounded disgusted that I would consider the thought that he wouldn't be on my side.

"Thanks buddy. But I need a breather. We'll be back in a little bit."

I gave him a good scratch behind the ears. "I love you, buddy. Thanks for protecting the house."

It's my job.

"Enjoy your kitty treats." I stood up.

First, Ozzy would get a nice long walk and then I needed

to talk to Aerie. Since my sister had come to town, I was definitely getting my exercise. At least Ozzy was happy about it. She bounced up and down as we left the house and I thought how nice it would be to be a pet and not have to talk to one's sister ever again.

8

———

For as much as Aerie had been fan-girling on Darla, I wondered where her loyalties lay. I shook it off. With me, of course. Right?

Leave it to Darla to make me second-guess every single aspect of my life.

I walked around to cool off. Ozzy was more than happy. The afternoon heat still radiated off the sidewalk. I made my way to the post office and the bank. I continued past the police station to the general store. I had it in my head I would buy myself a bottle of water there, but I didn't want to be social. I carried Ozzy with me and walked to the back of the store and grabbed a bottle of water. I smiled at Mr. Hooper as he rang up my bill.

"Hot enough for ya out there? I'm looking forward to heading to the lake this weekend."

"That's a good idea, Mr. Hooper. I hope you have a great time." He handed back my card, and I put it inside my phone case. Standing outside the store, I took a long sip of water and exhaled. Ozzy and I made a loop. We crossed the street, walked back towards the diner and Aerie's house.

I climbed the steps of her front stoop and knocked on the door. Aerie opened with a bright grin that slowly faded as she saw my face, or maybe my aura. "What's wrong?"

"Can I come in?" I glanced down at Ozzy.

"Yes, of course." She ushered me into the kitchen. She left me at the table while she put her cat into the bathroom. It was for Snowball's own mental health. Ozzy's level of excitement was a little too much for Aerie's high-strung kitty. I took the leash off Ozzy, rolled it up like a tape measure, and set it on the table. Then I laid my head down on my arms. Things had been looking good between me and my sister. Things had been looking good between me and Dan. And now it was a huge train wreck.

"Tell me what's going on."

I explained to her everything, including the slight case of breaking and entering that led to Arnold discovering our first real clue. But I also explained how Dan and Darla were conspiring against me and that I could no longer trust either of them.

"Wow. That's rough."

"No kidding."

"I suppose your date with Dan is off then, huh?"

I just stared at her, blank-faced.

"I thought so. That's too bad. I had hopes for you guys."

"It never would have worked out anyway. He's too straightlaced and I'm...not."

"There is always my brother," she joked.

I put my head back down and talked into the table. "Aerie, I'm not sure you realize this, but your brother has been in a serious relationship with Chelsea for more than four months. I don't think that status is going to change anytime soon."

"A girl can dream." No love was lost between Aerie and

Chelsea. Chelsea may have told Jay that she had mended her snarky, bullying ways but both Aerie and I knew better from experience.

"Do you know what I think you should do?"

"What? I'm all ears."

"I think you should solve this case."

"You're kidding. Why?"

"So you can show Darla and Dan how brilliant you are and how you can handle things on your own."

I let a small grin show up on my face. "Yeah. I wouldn't mind doing that. It would prove to them I don't need a babysitter." I shifted in the chair. "I'm certainly not going to talk to either of them again. Luckily, I have this." I pulled out my phone and showed her the photos I had taken of the encrypted piece of paper.

"You know who would be able to help us with this?"

"Ellie?" Ellie was twenty-something and dating a known computer hacker. She also had her own set of unique, and occasionally illegal, skills.

"Yep, and I know for a fact she'll be at the carnival this evening."

"We can always stop by her place between the breakfast and lunch rush tomorrow."

"Or we could go to the carnival, interview more potential suspects, and try to find her now." Aerie handed back my phone.

"I like the way you think, Aerie." I stood, putting my lemonade glass in her sink. "Let's go."

It was still early for the carnival when we got up there. Aerie had let me leave Ozzy at her place. I absolutely did not want to see Darla right now.

We scanned the crowds for Ellie, but she was nowhere in sight.

We now knew from Dan that the victim had worked at the carnival. It made sense for Aerie and I to walk around and get a feel for some of the other workers here. We had already talked to the strongman, Tony, so we didn't feel like we needed to interview him again. But Aerie had other plans.

"He was really cute. We could ask again if he knows anything. It couldn't hurt."

"Stop trying to set me up. It's not a good idea." We continued our walk up the hill. "In my current state of mind, I wouldn't trust my actions."

"Why? Would you become a suspect?"

"It's a high possibility."

"Noted. But I still want to talk to Tony again." She waggled her eyebrows.

"You're dating Sam. And he's a darling."

"I'm not saying I want to have a relationship with Tony. He's just nice on the eyes."

"Sometimes you frighten me."

"I like to keep you on your toes." She took my elbow, and we quickened our pace toward the carnival entrance. "It'll be good for you," she said.

Once I saw the carnival lights, I realized if things had gone differently this afternoon, I would have been there on a date with Dan. I balked. "I'm kind of hungry. Maybe we should do this at another time."

"Oh no, you don't." Her fingers gripped my forearm. "We're going in there to do some interviewing. When you fall off the horse you get back on." She marched me onto the carnival grounds. "Come on, we can throw darts at some balloons. You can pretend they're Dan's face."

I actually liked that idea. "Let's do it."

I was on a mission. A mission to vent some frustration and anger. And pop a few balloons. Aerie guided me straight to the dart-throwing booth. The woman who stood in the booth had dirty blond hair and a two-pocket apron. She blew up balloons and tied them with an expertise and speed that came from years of practice.

"I don't have them all up ladies, but I bet one of you could win yourself a prize." Aerie's grin was all she needed for encouragement. "Five dollars for three tries. Here's the darts."

I knew how this worked. As soon as one of us touched those darts, we had to pay for them.

She handed me three darts. I reached into my phone to get the bill.

"No, no, it's on me. Aerie slammed a five-dollar bill on the counter and the woman snatched it up in a heartbeat and stuffed it in her apron.

"Good luck. You pop one balloon to get the small stuffed prize, pop two, and you get a mouse, and pop three, and you get the grand prize hanging up there at the top." She pointed to a large stuffed purple cow hanging above the booth.

"You're kidding, right? Actual mice?" That was all I needed. I had been picking up pets like nobody's business since I moved to Pleasant Pond and it really had to stop somewhere.

The woman pointed to a hand-drawn sign at the side of the booth. One Win: Small Stuffed Animal. Two Wins: ~~Medium Stuffed Animal~~ A Mouse. Three Wins: Giant Prize.

"The idiot who runs the Tent of Terror left Perry the Python's food to their own devices and they mated. A lot.

"So, if you don't give them away..." Aerie let the sentence drift off. I was sure she didn't want to hear the answer.

"Perry will become an overweight python." The woman grinned.

"Mira, win a mouse!"

I was torn. I didn't need any more pets, but my competitive nature won out. I'd try my best to save a mouse or two. I planted my feet like I knew what I was doing, which I didn't. The first dart swirled from my fingers. It hit the board flat and dropped to the ground like a rock.

The woman took this opportunity to teach me a few things about dart throwing. "You planted your feet, that's good. Now hold the dart like you're holding a pencil. Good. Now bring it up near your ear and throw it like you're pointing at the balloon."

I threw the second dart. It popped the blue balloon near the center of the board.

"Woo hoo!" Aerie jumped up and down. "You did it!"

I grinned. I did. Halfway to saving a mouse. I had one more dart and this time the balloon that I was aiming for was Dan's head. I planted my feet, pinched the dart, pulled back to my ear, let it fly. This time the dart sank deeply into the cork board. Drat. And also, thank goodness. No extra pets.

"Good try, you almost had it. Three more tries?"

"No, I think we're done." I could easily see us wasting tens of dollars here with my need to bash something. And if I got really good at it, I'd have to start a pet store.

The woman pulled down a bin full of little stuffed purple cows and handed me one. "Here you go. Be sure to come back and try again. You have a great arm."

"Thanks. What's your name?"

"Jessie. Nice to meet you." She held out her arm. And I shook it. She had quite a strong grip. And I noticed her biceps and forearm flexing. I had no doubt that this woman had set up her own booth.

As we walked away, I asked Aerie, "You didn't want to have a try?"

"No. I figure we'll head over to Sam's later and get some pizza and we can practice dart throwing there for free."

"Good idea." I could tell Aerie was thinking we'd get good at darts and come back to liberate Perry's extra snacks.

"But first let's go talk to Tony."

"You know you are crazy, right?"

"Humor me," she said.

"Fine." Maybe we could find out some more about the murder victim now that we knew his name. Maybe Tony knew who he was. Suddenly all I wanted was to see Tony with his hammer. And fine biceps.

When we got to the strong man's booth, a long line of middle school kids were trying their might with the hammer. Tony gave advice on how to put their weight behind it, and he hit the bell himself a couple times to prove his point. It was impressive. I felt like I could watch him heft that hammer all day long. But we couldn't very well grill him with all the kids around.

Aerie had the same thought. "Let's get some tickets and ride the teacups while we wait for this to clear up."

I couldn't remember the last time I had ridden the teacups anywhere, let alone at a carnival.

"Sure. I think the ticket booth is back over that way." We made our way to the stand where an older woman with curly white hair sat in the little glass box exchanging money for tickets. "I'm only buying enough tickets for this one ride.

I am hungry. After we talk to Tony, I'd really love to get some pizza."

"I hear you. I haven't seen Sam all day."

The old lady smiled at me as she handed me the tickets. "Have fun, young lady."

"Thanks, I will." We wandered toward the rides.

No one stood in line at the teacups, since the ride sat at the very back of the carnival and it was still relatively early in the evening. Things would pick up once it got dark and the high school kids filed in.

The ride monitor stood at the controls looking bored. I took that as an opening. "Is it always slow this early?"

"Yeah, once it gets dark is when everyone shows up. You two want a ride?"

"Sure. Hey, would you happen to know a Joel Bauer?"

Aerie gave me a knowing look. She knew I couldn't give up investigating.

"Nope," he said, and his face closed up. "Can't say that I do." He wouldn't look me in the eye after that, so Aerie and I turned and walked through the ride entrance.

"I always want to sit in the red cup." Aerie pulled me in that direction.

"Why?" We climbed inside and sat down. We attached the leash-like seatbelts.

"I think it spins faster."

This could be a bad idea. The ride started with a slow turn. I reminded myself that at least I hadn't eaten dinner yet. It picked up speed. Aerie had a sweet yet maniacal grin on her face. She reached forward and took the center wheel in both hands and pulled hard to turn it. Our teacup began to spin. I might as well join in. "I bet we can get this to really spin." I placed my hands in between hers and together we tugged and turned the wheel until the outside world was a blur. We continued to pull on the center disk, trying our best to make it go faster and faster. Then, slowly the ride decelerated, and we sat with our heads spinning instead.

"That was fun." I stood and swayed.

"See?" She laughed.

"Yes. It was fun."

"Want to go again?"

"Nope." I snorted. But I had to admit it took my mind off everything, at least for a moment. "Let's go talk to our friend Tony; obviously people here know the victim. I gripped the side of the teacup in an attempt to regain my balance and headed toward the back of the ride where a sign said, Exit.

"No, this way." Aerie pointed me in the right direction, and we headed out. My head was seriously still spinning until we got past the carousel.

"See, I told you, you would have fun on the ride."

"It was fun. For the two and half minutes that the ride ran, I temporarily forgot about Darla and Dan's complete and utter betrayal of my trust."

"Bitter."

"Absolutely." We made our way towards the booths. We looked high and low for Ellie, but while we saw people from town we recognized, Ellie wasn't one of them.

You could spot Tony's strong man area from anywhere at the carnival. The twenty-foot-tall tower had a set of lights that blinked even before the evening hours had the rest of the carnival lit up. The crowd we had seen earlier had dissipated and Tony stood organizing his shelf of prizes.

Aerie was quick to step up and talk to Tony. "Hey, Tony, remember us?"

He glanced at Aerie, but his eyes rested on me. "I remember you." A smile played at the corner of his lips. "You were *this* close to hitting the bell. I could feel it." He winked at me. It was so comical I blurted out in a laugh. Aerie witnessed this exchange. "Mira, here, is getting over a boyfriend issue. She was supposed to be here on a carnival date with a guy tonight, but instead is here with me."

I shot her an I-can't-believe-you-just-said-that glance.

Tony's focus was now completely on me. It was as if Aerie was no longer there.

"Would you consider going out with me on that date?" He was actually nervous. "If you can be here tomorrow evening, someone can take over my spot and I will show you the carnival and all its secrets." He grinned, his salesman-like persona was gone and he was just a guy asking out a girl.

Before I could even realize it, I said, "Yes." He looked so sweet and happy and I didn't mind those biceps either. "So, see you tomorrow?"

"Will seven work for you?"

"Sure."

"Great. See you then." Then he actually blushed. It made me smile.

Aerie grabbed my arm and hustled me away. She leaned close. "Great job. Now we can really find out what's going on."

Confused for a second, I actually forgot all about the investigation for the duration that Tony had his eyes on me. I cleared my throat. "Yeah. The date is totally to get information from him."

"Now let's head over to Sam's and eat some pizza."

"I heartily agree. I am starving." Nobody could beat Sam's pizza.

"I need to practice my dart throwing."

9

———

Aerie drove us out to the strip mall where the Pizza Pub, the restaurant and bar that Sam owned, was located. As soon as I opened the car door, I smelled the oven baked pizza and my mouth watered. Of course, when we got inside, Aerie and Sam exchanged hugs and kisses. They were so cute together.

Sam held Aerie at arm's length. "Are you alright? I heard you two were at the flea market when the murder happened?"

"I'm fine, we're fine. Mira found the body, but we weren't able to learn much else."

Sam chuckled. "Unfazed by death, my girlfriend hunts for clues."

Aerie swooned. "I love when you say that."

"That you're my girlfriend, or the word *clues*?" he said, playfully.

She pulled away but held his hand. "Girlfriend, silly."

"It's the clues." Sam nodded with a grin and returned to swirling sauce on a pizza crust.

We each ordered our own small pizzas. Aerie asked for

a vegan pie. I requested extra onions and mushrooms. Once we climbed into a booth, Aerie asked, "Can I see the photos you have of the piece of paper that was in the desk?"

I pulled out my phone, in a few clicks I found the photos and expanded them to fill the screen. I handed it to her. She held the phone close to her face, squinting at the symbols. "Do you know what it is?"

"You mean the code it's written in? Nope. Do you have any ideas?"

"No. But I think you're right, we should bring it over to Ellie. She has a whole network of internet friends that might be able to figure it out."

I nodded. Besides being the town's excellent source of gossip, Ellie's obsession with the internet and hacking often came in handy.

Our pizzas showed up, and I was hungry enough to devour every last bite.

After we finished eating, Aerie and I played darts, measuring the distance so it was similar to the balloon booth. We nursed our sodas and threw darts, making small talk with Sam between orders, until finally Aerie felt confident she could win at the dart booth. Aerie and Sam said their goodbyes. Sam wished me luck on my date with Tony. I half-grinned and shook my head.

As we got into the car to go home a thought came to me. "Hey, Aerie?"

"Yeah?"

"Don't mention my date with Tony to Dan if you talk to him." Only a tiny part of me felt like I was cheating or something.

"The last thing I'm going to do is let him in on our investigation. I don't plan on talking to him anytime soon."

"Or my sister, okay?" The last thing I needed was my sister giving me more unsolicited advice.

"Sure, okay. No worries. I won't say a word."

"Because they'll think I'm just doing it to spite them."

"Aren't you?"

"No, actually I thought Tony was very sweet."

"You're not investigating him as a suspect for murder?"

"No. Well, maybe. Both. He's sweet and might have information. But do you think he could have done it?"

"I think you should keep that in the back of your mind. As nice as he looks, and as nice as he is, he could still be our killer."

"Yeah, you're right. I'll keep it in mind."

By the time I picked up Ozzy from Aerie's house and got home, my sister had gone to bed. Or at least she was in her room with the door closed. I was glad we wouldn't have to have a conversation. I still didn't know what I would say to her. My life was finally going in a decent direction and she managed to screw it up. Whatever. I needed to let that go for now. Tomorrow I had a date with a potential killer, albeit sweet. A very strong, muscular possible killer. I had to remind myself of that. I needed to plan out how I would get information from him in a subtle enough way that he wouldn't realize it. But that was for tomorrow. Once my head hit the pillow, I felt little kitty paws traipse across the bed and curl up above my head.

Did you have onions for dinner?

"Yes, go to sleep, Arnold."

THE NEXT MORNING, I was out of the house before my sister woke. Instead of going to yoga class, I went straight to the diner and began setting up for the morning rush. I figured the more things we had in place, the sooner we could get a chance to run over and see Ellie between breakfast and lunch.

The morning rush went smoothly enough. Both Dan and my sister came in at different points and quietly ordered and left with takeout. Aerie let me know about it because I refused to come out of the kitchen. I wasn't ready to talk to either of them yet.

After the dining room cleared from breakfast, I helped Aerie bus the tables and clean up so we could run over to visit Ellie at her job at the bank.

As always, the air conditioning was cranked to an unbelievable level. The lobby itself felt like an igloo. Ellie was busy typing away on her computer at her teller window. When she saw us, she waved us over. "Tell me. Tell me. All about the murder. What did you guys see? I heard you were the first ones there. Did you take any photos?"

"No, Ellie, we don't have photos. Not of the crime scene, anyway. But I do have pictures of something else I want you to look at."

"Really?"

"Maybe you can help us with this. I think it's a clue, but it's in some kind of code."

"Ooh, a cipher? I love that stuff." Ellie was emphatic. She desperately wanted to see the photos I had. I pulled them up on my phone and handed it to her. After a few seconds she asked, "Can I print these out?"

I hesitated for a minute, but I didn't see a problem with it. It was probably better than me texting it to her. With a known hacker as a boyfriend, who knew what government agency would be interested in her texts? "I don't see any reason why not. But keep this under wraps. It's considered evidence."

Aerie nodded her head knowingly. "Dan would probably get pretty upset if he knew."

Ellie was on board with the whole thing. "As soon as I figure this out, I will let you guys know."

"Thanks Ellie, we really appreciate it."

"Now can you tell me about the murder?"

"Sorry, we need to head back to the diner. Plus, all we did was find a dead guy. Nothing to tell."

"You just don't want to talk about dead people."

"That's my sister's domain, talking about and to dead people."

She pouted for a second but then looked down at the printout that she held. "Thanks for giving me something fun to do today. I'm excited to figure this out. I'll text you guys."

Aerie and I left to get back to Soup and Scoop. The diner was still quiet and dark. I noticed someone standing outside the door, waiting.

As we got closer, I realized it was Alex...stupid, ex-boyfriend, Alex. "What is he doing here?"

When I got close enough, I put my hands on my hips. "What are you doing here, Alex?"

He grinned that rakish boyish grin that sucked me in the first time I met him. "You sell burgers here, right? And fries?"

By this time Aerie had unlocked the door, and Alex followed her inside. I ignored him and went straight to the kitchen where I turned on the fryer, fired up the grill, and began prep for the lunch rush. Aerie came in a few minutes later. "Hamburger and fries. I'll get the strawberry shake."

I remained focused on the grill. I didn't even want to

look in the direction of the dining room. "Make sure he shows you his cash first."

"That bad, huh?"

"There's a reason I never talk about him."

"I think I'm going to need to hear this story, over wine or something."

"Yeah, but not right now. I'll make his burger and his fries. But I'm not kidding about asking to see his cash first."

Aerie giggled. "Okay." She turned around and went back out to the dining room.

I quickly fried up his burger, mad at myself that I knew exactly how he liked it. I slid the fries on the plate, cramming them next to the hamburger. I decided to take it directly to him. I needed to know why he was here.

I walked out to the dining room to see him sucking down the strawberry shake Aerie had made.

"Did Aerie ask to see your cash? Because if she didn't, I want to make sure you're paying for this meal. I'm done paying for you."

"Take a step back, girlfriend. I have my own money." He reached into his back pocket flashing a wad of twenties.

"You'd have to tip me a hundred times more than what you have in that wallet to make amends for how much you took from me."

"Look, Mira, I owed some sketchy people some money. You happened to have some. For which I am still very grateful."

I gave him the evil eye. "Why are you here?"

"Luck, if you believe that." He stuck a french fry in his mouth and chewed.

"I don't believe that. Why are you here?"

"Let me take you out so we can talk about it."

"On what planet do you think I would ever date you again?"

"You know you can't resist me." He leaned casually forward and flashed his sparkling grin.

"That's a deficit I've gotten over." I felt the muscle in my neck tightening up. It was like my previous life had crashed into Pleasant Pond, the haven I had moved to in order to escape that life. My no-good ex. My controlling sister. I just wanted them to leave me alone.

He shrugged nonchalantly. "Come on, you know you want to know what I've been up to. Maybe I could pay you back some of that cash I borrowed."

"Borrowed, my foot," I mumbled.

His dark hair fell over one eye and he pushed it back. "I see you got a nice house over there. You can't be doing too bad for yourself."

"You're not getting any of the little money I have left over after you swindled me. Don't get any ideas." I almost threw in that I knew the town's chief of police until the thought of Dan made me even madder.

"I don't want any of your money. Like I said, I have my own means these days." He took a bite of his burger. "Mmm, this is good. Who knew you were such a good cook?"

I was seconds away from reaching across the counter and punching him in that sexy, snarky mouth of his.

"I do care about you Mira, I just wanted to make sure that you were set up, you know taken care of, after everything."

"You mean after everything you did to me, like lying straight to my face and stealing my savings?"

"But not your heart?"

"My heart is dead to you."

"You know you want to brag to me about your new house. Why don't you show me around?"

"In your dreams." I turned to Aerie. "Make sure he pays before he leaves.

I gave him one last glaring look. "And you'd better tip well."

I grumbled as I walked back into the kitchen. Darla had mentioned something about her vision of seeing me have a problem with men in my life. I hated when Darla was right.

I STOOD in the middle of Aerie's bedroom pulling on a dress.

"But you have to go." Aerie looked up at me with imploring eyes.

"I don't really want to go on a date. Clearly, my luck with men ran out a long time ago." I let go of the zipper on the back of my dress and the ends hung open at my back.

"This isn't a real date."

"Yeah, yeah, I know." She was right. This date was all about gaining more information about people who worked at the carnival and what they knew about the guy in the blue baseball hat. "But it feels like a real one." I had refused to go home after closing up the diner. I didn't want to talk to Darla. So, I was trying on Aerie's summer dresses until I found one that she said was flattering.

"Just remember to ask questions like you usually do and if things get sketchy, text me, and I'll show up and rescue you."

I grinned at that. Our rescue attempts were always a bit interesting.

"Okay, just don't mention anything to Dan, even if it goes sideways."

"It won't. He'd probably throw me in the slammer for letting you go out with a potential suspect." She zipped up the back of the dress. "This one is it. You look great."

"Thanks."

"Okay, some lip gloss, a bit of bronzer." She had already whipped out a makeup bag and began to put items on the table. I had never seen her wear a stitch of makeup so I was in shock while she applied the bronzer lightly across my cheeks. "I had been hoping to do this for your date with Dan...but that will just have to be for another time I guess."

"Another time? I will never date someone who conspires with my sister. Nope. I've written him off."

Aerie sighed and shrugged. "Maybe. I'm still hoping to break up Jay and Chelsea and get you and my brother together."

"I don't see that happening any time soon." Jay visited less and less at my place now that the kitchen was sheet-rocked. I couldn't afford any cabinets or appliances yet anyway. He was busy splitting time between his construction company and building his own house, which he planned on sharing with Chelsea.

Aerie shook the gloss. "Just remember, ask about the guy in the blue hat, find out if he knew him, and how the flea market is connected." She tapped it lightly to my lips giving them a subtle shine.

I heard a knock at the door downstairs. "I wonder who that is?" Aerie left me in front of the mirror. She had done a great job of dressing me up, makeup and all. I looked like I had actually slept last night. And then I heard her voice.

"Is Mira here?" Darla was at the front door.

I went to the top of the stairs. "I don't want to talk about it, Darla," I shouted at the stairs.

"Can you please come down? I just want to apologize."

I felt like a pouting teenager as I descended the stairs. At least my feet looked good in a pair of Aerie's strappy sandals.

When I got to the bottom, Darla looked surprised. "Oh, you forgave Dan and you're going out tonight, that's good."

"No." I refused to elaborate.

"You're obviously going somewhere." She glanced at Aerie who still had her hair pulled back, and she was wearing the clothes she had on at the diner. "But not with Aerie."

"No." I glared at her. She didn't need to know what I was doing. "You came to apologize?" I stood straighter.

Darla held up her hand. "Hold on. Where are you going?"

"To the carnival."

"With whom?" Then she stopped herself. "I don't need to know. Just don't go. And I'll tell you why."

"Who says you get to tell me what to do anymore?"

"That's the whole reason I'm here, Mira. You can't trust any of the men you come in contact with this week."

"This is exactly why I moved here, Darla. I'm tired of being told what to do."

"But I'm protecting you. Something bad is going to happen. Do you think I drove all the way from Massachusetts just to say, 'hi'?"

"I don't care Darla, I'm going out."

"Please don't. I'm sorry for asking Dan to look after you. I shouldn't have done that. But please listen to me now. Something bad is going to go down. I can't see what it is, but it would be best if you stayed home." Her face had that desperate look, the one that used to make my resolution cave. I stood strong.

"It's my life. I get to decide what to do with it." I glanced over at Aerie. "Thanks for helping me get dressed. I'll text you later." I stuffed my cell phone in the front pocket of the sundress and walked out Aerie's front door.

This was how it always worked. We were back to our same old same old. Darla would tell me what not to do and I would go ahead and do it anyway. This usually ended in spectacular disaster. Like dating a guy who ended up stealing my savings. Well, I had a job to do. I needed to investigate the suspects at the carnival. And if it was under the pretense of a date, so be it. I had my cell phone. I could take care of myself.

TONY HAD ASKED that I meet him at his high striker station. Sure enough, when I got there, he was demonstrating how to hit the striker hard enough to ring the bell. With his shirt off. I was only slightly upset when he noticed me and, with a big grin, pulled on a black T-shirt.

"Hi, Mira. I hope your day was good?"

His joy was infectious, and I easily forgot about the argument with my sister. "It was good." My hands were sweating. Why was I so nervous?

He rubbed his large hands together. "I'm excited to show you the carnival. I'll even share some of it secrets." He winked. "Where would you like to go first?"

"Oh, I don't know. What's your favorite ride?"

"It's not really a ride, does that count?"

"Sure."

"The haunted mansion."

"Yeah?" For some reason it surprised me that this big guy loved the scary mansion. "What do you like about it?"

"First, it's mysterious when you walk up to the front

door, you're not sure what you're getting into. But then once you are inside, things change. You don't know where to go and you have to figure it out. It's fun."

"Let's go see it."

"Great." As we passed a lemonade stand, Tony asked, "Do you want something to drink?"

"Sure." I reached into my pocket and pulled out my phone where I stored my cash.

Tony waved at me. "No, no, I've got it." He grinned and ordered us two large lemonades.

"Thanks." I took a long sip. The fresh sour citrus mixed with the crunch of the granulated sugar swirled in my mouth as I gulped it down. "I forgot how good these were."

"Sherry makes a mean lemonade." He smiled and winked at her. She smiled. We crossed the grounds toward the haunted house at the back of the property, sipping our iced confections. I had to force myself to remember this guy was a murder suspect.

"You're sure it's not too scary?"

I looked up at the blackened exterior of the haunted house. I knew they unpacked this at each new venue. It wasn't a real haunted house. Like mine. I let out a laugh. "Sorry. I didn't mean to laugh at the haunted house." The confused look on Tony's face forced me to explain. "I was just thinking this isn't a real haunted house, like my own house."

"Your house is haunted?"

"Pretty much."

"Does that scare you?"

"No. The ghost and I came to an agreement." He nodded like he understood.

"This haunted house is really just for fun." He took my

hand in his, which surprised me, but I found it oddly reassuring. "Let me show you the trick."

I was a little concerned about what this trick might be, because he was a murder suspect and all, but my curiosity won out. I followed Tony into the dark haunted house.

The fog machine was running overtime and I couldn't see my feet, but I could feel the cold mist as it hovered around my ankles. The first few steps into the house were eerily quiet. Someone deeper inside screamed, and I jumped.

Tony gripped my hand gently. "Come on," he whispered. The scream melted into laughter and I relaxed slightly.

The hall we walked down was narrow and dark with strobe lights flashing up ahead.

"Close your eyes."

"What?" I wasn't sure if I wanted to do that. My nerves were on high alert.

He gripped my hand. "Trust me, close your eyes."

Did I trust him? That was the question. Darla had said not to trust any men I met this week, so, to spite her, I closed my eyes and let Tony pull me through the hallway.

Someone screamed from behind, and I jumped again.

Tony held my hand firmly. "Go ahead, now you can open them."

I blinked my eyes open, and found we were in a dimly lit room full of mirrors. The two of us appeared to be in the center with thousands of copies of us getting smaller and smaller.

Tony smiled. "Cool, right?"

I turned in a circle and joined him with a grin. The sparkly hair clip Aerie gave me shined back a thousand times. "Very cool."

He offered me his hand again and I took it. "You can't

really see it as well if you had your eyes open past the strobe lights. That's the trick."

I glanced around. "How do we get out?"

"Ah, easy enough. You can always look on the floor to see where the paint is worn, then you'll know the path out, but..." he raised a finger, "there's another secret to this haunted house." His grin widened.

"You look like you're about to show me."

"Do you want to see it? It might ruin the haunting experience."

"I'll risk it."

"Okay, follow me." He turned and I walked behind him, admiring his broad muscular back.

Again, he pulled me through the hallways, left then right, then left again. Spooky spiders hung from the ceiling and a vampire stood in a coffin propped in the corner. The floor inclined as we walked. I wondered if we were headed to the second floor. Then the hallway opened up and I watched Tony wave to a shadowed figure hidden off to the side, who nodded. We passed the shadow and continued through the dark room. A shiver ran down my spine. I took a deep breath. What could happen in a carnival prop? I followed Tony who still held my hand. He stopped abruptly and I ran smack into his muscle-toned back. His cologne was intoxicating.

"Sorry. I should have warned you." He said. He let go of my hand.

I scrunched my eyes closed. When I opened them, he was gone. I took a step forward in the dark. Nothing. I turned around. Nothing.

Something grabbed my wrist. I screamed and practically jumped out of my skin. The hand pulled me firmly past the black scrim and suddenly I was outside staring up at Tony's face. "What happened?" I asked.

"There's a door behind the curtain." We stood on a platform attached to the back of the haunted house. "It's the emergency exit."

It was quiet back here, where the carnival met the edge of a field merging into the woods behind. A slow breeze blew from the forest and cooled the nervousness from the back of my neck. I looked up at Tony. "It's really nice back here." And oddly romantic.

He nodded and took a step closer. He rested his hand on my hip and leaned down the littlest bit as if to kiss me. "The carnival holds more secrets."

I gulped. "Okay." Tony turned and started down the iron stairs and I found I could breathe again.

Get it together, Mira, the hot guy doesn't want to kill you. It's just a date. I took a deep breath.

Tony leaned on the railing at the base of the stairs waiting for me. "What would you like to do next?" he asked. "Have you eaten dinner? I can ask Sue to make us a couple of her peppers and sausages."

My stomach growled at the thought. "That sounds great." I could use a bite to eat to settle my nerves.

Tony walked next me but gave me my space as we headed towards the row of food kiosks at the center of the carnival grounds. I caught sight of a skulking figure behind the fried Twinkie booth. Aerie twiddled her fingers at me in a silent "hello." My sister stood behind her. What were they up to?

I glared at the two of them, hoping, pleading that they would just go home. Tony noticed my glare so I figured now was as good a time as any for me to start asking questions. "You seem to know everybody here at the carnival."

"I've worked here for years. Ever since I was twelve? Yeah, I think that's right, twelve."

"Wow, that's pretty young."

"My family owns it. So, I help run it."

"Oh. I didn't know you were in charge."

"I don't like to put on airs like I own the place. Everybody here contributes a huge amount to keep this carnival running. I just make sure everyone gets paid on time." We made our way to the food trailers. And waited in line for a few moments until a woman leaned out the window. "Tony, over here." She waved us to the open window. "Introduce me, Tony?" she asked with a huge smile on her lined face.

"This is Mira. I'm showing her around tonight."

"Now don't share all the secrets." But she smiled like she knew that's exactly what Tony planned to do. "Now what can I get you two?"

"Two of your best, Sue." Tony turned to me. "Are you okay with peppers and onions?"

"I love them."

"Got it. Two of the best with peppers and onions coming right up."

While we waited, Tony pulled two napkins out of the dispenser for each of us, folded them and handed me a neatly folded square. By the time he was done, Sue propped the window open again. "Here you go." She handed Tony two paper plates with long rolls covered in peppers and onions. My mouth watered at the scent of the roasted sausage.

"Would you like to sit at a picnic table or out in the field?"

While the idea of sitting in the field was somewhat romantic, my sundress would make it awkward. And with messy sausage sandwiches? "Picnic table. They're back this way, right?"

He nodded and I led the way, pulling out my phone and quickly texting Aerie, I refused to acknowledge my sister. *Go home, I'm fine.*

Once I sat down, Tony handed me my plate. "Thank you." I waited until he sat next to me. "This is fun, Tony. Thank you for inviting me."

I furtively glanced around. Aerie and Darla had disappeared. My phone buzzed. My sister texted back: *Be careful.* I sighed and focused on the food in front of me.

"Good to hear. I have more fun stuff planned after we eat." He looked as intent on his sandwich as I did. I attempted to be polite and dainty while eating but when that obviously wasn't happening, I dug in. I glanced over at Tony. He managed to eat the entire thing in four bites. Like a pro, he wasn't covered in onions and peppers like I was. He dabbed his lips with the napkin a few times but that was it. I practically needed a shower; I was covered in all the greasy juices from a miraculous sandwich. Tony watched with humor in his eyes as I made a mess of myself.

After my last bite, I leaned forward. "Do you think Sue could come to the diner and show me how she made these?"

"You work at a diner?"

"Oh, yeah. Sorry. I'm the cook at one here in town."

"Then Sue would be thrilled to hear that the chef at the local diner is impressed with her subs."

I nodded enthusiastically. "This is the best sausage sandwich ever."

After I cleaned myself with a thousand paper napkins, he asked, "Do you want to head over to the carousel? I can show you which one is my favorite since I was a kid."

"I'd love it. Any secrets I should know about?"

"Nope. I figured it would be easier on us with full stomachs to take it slow before we attempt any of the other rides."

"Smart thinking." We got up from the table, disposed of the plates and napkins, and walked to the large carousel that sat at the end of the row of food trailers. But instead of going right to the carousel Tony walked past it toward the ticket booth. I assumed he was going to buy tickets. But when the old woman opened the window, Tony grinned. "Granny, I want you to meet someone."

"What did I tell you about calling me Granny?" the old lady reprimanded.

"This is Mira." He proudly presented me to the lady I assumed was his grandmother. Oh, was I already meeting the family?

"She doesn't want to meet me. Go take her on some rides and show her a good time." She leaned forward to close the window. "Nice to meet you, Mira. Go have fun."

Tony smiled and turned, walking towards the carousel. "That's my Gran. But she hates when I point that out."

"Women like to keep their age a secret."

Tony gave me an inquisitive look.

"Nope. Not saying."

"Fine with me. That way we can ride on the carousel just like kids."

A warm flush came over me. No, I was not falling for Tony. But man, he was sweet and I really wanted to. But I reminded myself again: he was a suspect. Everyone who worked here was. Well, maybe not Granny.

Once the carousel stopped and the children departed, he hopped onto the platform and leaned down a hand to help me up. "Thanks." He was chivalrous, too. We walked about a third of the way around the carousel. Each animal appeared to be hand carved wood painted in layers of gleaming vibrant paint. Little kids ran past us, and Tony leaned out of their way and laughed as they passed. "I'm not as fast as these little guys. Not anymore." He stopped at a racehorse that was frozen in mid-stride. Its black glossy coat shined under the lights. "This here is Mystic, the best horse around." Tony ran his hand along the side affectionately. "I used to pretend I was a cowboy in the old West."

A little boy screeched to a halt right in front of Tony. He looked up at Tony with huge brown eyes.

"You want to ride this one?" Tony asked.

The little guy nodded. "Need a help up?" Tony glanced around for a parent. The mom, behind him, nodded. Tony picked up the little boy and placed him on the horse. "This is Mystic, you take good care of him now." The little boy nodded with a huge grin on his face as he took the reins.

Tony smiled. "Come on, I have a place for us to sit."

I followed Tony as we wound our way to a covered bench seat behind what looked like an ostrich and an African lion. He offered for me to sit down first. Again, the gentleman. I couldn't get over how kind he was. He sat next to me. The bench was small, and Tony was a big guy, so his thigh pressed against mine. This really was a date. I might want to find out more information about the carnival, but right now I decided to live in the moment. Tony was polite, sweet, and beyond sexy. The night was beautiful with a cool breeze, children were laughing, and the lights sparkled overhead.

And then I wrecked it. "Tony, do you know anything about the guy in the blue hat, because he broke into my house the other day."

"He what?" He growled.

"Yeah. I don't think he took anything but I'm wondering

if he had anything to do with Joel Bauer's death."

Tony tensed. "I know I said earlier, I didn't know him, but I was just trying to keep the carnival secrets to ourselves —the real ones. We're pretty private. But if people working for us start messing with the towns we stay in? That's not okay. I haven't seen him since we found out about Joel." He clenched his right fist in his lap. "I'll keep an eye out for him. He shouldn't be breaking into your house like that."

"Thanks. Sorry I brought it up."

"No, I'm glad you mentioned it. I'll take care of it; he won't bother you again." He smiled and patted my leg gently. The ride slowed and Tony stood. "Come on, let's have some more fun before it gets too late."

I stood and he helped me down off the side of the carousel.

"Are you up for a ride on the Ferris wheel?" He pointed toward the glowing circle of lights that pulsed and changed colors in different patterns.

I nodded. "I've always wanted to get a better view of the town."

He offered me his hand again. I took it. I hadn't ruined the evening like I thought.

As we walked, I decided right now, here, I didn't need to know anything about the guy in the blue hat. All I needed was this. This date. This nice guy holding my hand, about to ride the Ferris wheel like a couple of teenagers. I was loving every second of it.

We walked up the ramp to claim a seat. Tony held open the gate for me and I walked ahead. I tucked the sundress under me and sat on the cool metal seat. Tony sat next to me. Again, his leg brushed mine. A zing like electricity ran up my spine.

The ride monitor latched the bar across our seat.

"Thanks, Jim." Tony turned to me. "The Ferris wheel was also one of my favorites. When I was little, I had never been in a plane. I figured this was what it would look like being up so high."

The Ferris wheel lurched back and began its clockwise spin upward. After all the seats were filled, the Ferris wheel went around a full rotation. I noticed farmer Miller's land on the other side of the trees behind the haunted house. I could see the new hen houses that Jay had built there not too long ago. I looked across the town at how green and beautiful it was with the houses nestled together, creating the town of Pleasant Pond that I called home.

The Ferris wheel came to a stop when we were at the very top. Tony grinned at me. "The inside secret about the Ferris wheel is that you just have to give Jim a wink and he'll make sure to stop the wheel at the top." He looked out over the town. "Do you like it?"

"I love it. It's beautiful."

"So are you," he whispered.

I turned and found myself staring into his dark eyes.

"Can I kiss you?" he whispered again as I stared intently at his lips. I leaned into him. Once our lips met, I felt as if I were falling, dizzy and disoriented in all the best ways. Finally, we both took a breath and Tony sat back, taking my hand as I leaned my head against his shoulder.

"I'm having a really nice evening," I said.

"Good. That was my plan." He kissed the top of my head and the Ferris wheel started up again.

I FLOATED on a cloud of blissful happiness the entire walk home. When I got to my front door the only thing I could think about was the next time I would see Tony.

As if on cue, the universe laughed in my face. Alex and the dude in the blue hat were on my porch not-so-stealthily trying to figure out how to get in. No way. I stomped over to the porch. "What are you two doing here?"

They were so engrossed in their argument they hadn't heard me coming. Two shocked faces, like deer in the headlights, turned and stared at me. Then they both jumped off the porch and ran.

"I'm calling the cops," I shouted after them. Then I reconsidered. I really didn't want to call Dan. Then he would get the chance to be all protective like my sister had asked. And I could take care of myself. Even if my no-good thieving ex and a possible murderer had just been plotting on my porch. The last thing I wanted was to give my sister the satisfaction that I needed her foresight and Dan's protection. Because I didn't. I marched into the house. It might not be the smartest decision, but where my sister was concerned, sometimes smart flew the coop and I settled on stubborn.

I checked the first floor, locking every door and window tight. I threw the blanket over Taco's cage for the night and turned off the lights. The shock of seeing those idiots on my porch faded as I gave Ozzy a rubdown. It was okay that she wasn't a great watchdog. She followed me upstairs, and I eyed the closed door to the guest room. At first I thought Darla was on one of her client calls but then I heard Arnold purring his approval at something. And then I heard Darla, "Romantic relationships are so challenging. I thought coming here would help. But it feels like I am just running away."

Arnold purred.

"It must be nice being a consummate bachelor, Arnold."

Keep scratching, right there behind the ear... About that. I'm madly in love with a show cat. We're expecting kittens any day now.

"Well, you're not much of a comfort," Darla grumbled.

Personally, I believe in the phrase "just do it."

I snorted a laugh. That's how we ended up responsible for vet bills and kittens. Darla came to the door and opened it to find me looking guilty in the hall with Ozzy.

"How was your date?" She leaned against the door.

"It was good." I cleared my throat.

"I know that look." She shook her head. "Just don't get caught up with this guy, okay?"

"Darla, this is my own life, remember?"

"Right. Sorry. Sleep well." Her grin was tired.

I felt bad about her having to sleep on the cot. "It's still nice to have you here."

She had a tired grin as she closed the door.

I turned to find Arnold following Ozzy and me into the bedroom.

"What was that conversation with Darla about?"

She needed advice on a potential mate.

"She's dating someone?"

I don't understand this "dating".

"Yeah, yeah. I know your motto. 'Just do it.'" I shook my head.

As I got ready for bed, my thoughts drifted back to the wonderful night at the carnival. Remembering the kiss with Tony gave me a thrill down to my toes. Tomorrow I'd figure out what Alex was doing with the guy in the blue hat. And tomorrow I'd tell Aerie all about it. I hopped into bed and cuddled up to Arnold. Right now, I was looking forward to some peaceful dreams that hopefully involved Tony.

10

———

The next morning, I slipped out of the house without making any noise that would alert Darla that I was leaving. Although, she probably knew it, psychically. The bright daylight chased away any of my concerns over guys trying to break in to my house and I focused on how awesome last night's date was. My feet were still light as I walked into the diner. I had slept in and skipped yoga. Aerie was probably chomping at the bit to hear how the date went. And truth be told, I was eager to tell her all about it. I floated through opening the diner and prepping for breakfast. I had the grill and fryer heating when I heard the bells above the door chime.

Aerie came straight into the kitchen and grabbed her apron off its peg. "So, what did you find out about the murder?"

A little confused, I looked up from the griddle. "What?"

"Did you grill Tony and ask him about the guy in the blue hat?"

I took a deep breath and let it out slowly. "I had a wonderful date with Tony last night." I grinned

93

remembering. "He kissed me on the top of the Ferris wheel."

"You didn't ask him about the murder?"

"Way to kill the mood, Aerie." I turned and wiped down the counter. "Yes, I asked him. No, he doesn't know any more than he told us earlier. And I believe him."

"Is that why you let him kiss you at the top of the Ferris wheel?"

"Who kissed who at the top of the Ferris wheel?" called a deep and familiar voice from the dining room. My face flushed; my ears felt hot. Aerie looked at me, questioning.

I shook my head frantically and stayed in the kitchen. She went out to take Dan's breakfast order. I tried to get my breathing under control. Why did I care if Dan heard I'd kissed somebody last night? It was his fault I was on a date with someone else. I calmed myself down by prepping the rest of the breakfast items: pancake batter, the frozen sausages, the eggs from Miller's farm.

"It was stolen?" Aerie must've raised her voice just so I could hear. Curiosity got the best of me and I walked out to the dining room. "What was stolen?"

"Mr. Miller had an antique phonograph stolen from his house last night. And I hate to admit it, but the piece of evidence from that desk of yours was also stolen from our evidence locker."

"From the police station?" I blurted out.

Dan nodded reluctantly. "I wasn't at the station at the time. I can't understand how it was stolen, but it's gone." He took a sip of his coffee. "If either of you learn of anything..." He took a second to glance at me and then looked away quickly. "Can you let me know?"

"Yeah, sure." Then I remembered, "Last night Alex and the guy in the blue hat were at my house."

Dan became more alert and Aerie stared at me like I should have told her earlier. "I forgot." I shrugged. "But last night when I came home, Alex was with the guy in the blue hat on my back porch. They were arguing about something. I think they were trying to break in."

"And you didn't think to call the police station?" Dan practically shouted.

"No." I glared at him. "Besides, I chased them off. They knew I had seen them, so they weren't coming back."

Dan tensed in his seat. "You should have called the station. That man is wanted on suspicion of murder. Something could have happened to you."

"You're watching over me like my sister asked?" I squinted at him.

"Yes." He closed his eyes and took a deep breath. "No. I mean to say, you need to take this seriously. We don't know what the motive is. If he did murder someone, you could be at risk."

"Noted." Done with the conversation, I turned and walked back into the kitchen. I would let Aerie handle the hostess duties. I couldn't be around Dan without losing my temper.

The bell over the door chimed. I peeked out over the counter and saw Ellie. She looked a bit frazzled as she entered the diner. "Oh, Dan...Detective Lockheart. Some guy just tried to run me off the road on my way over here."

I listened as Ellie gave him details about the car's make and model. Ellie, of course, memorized everything. Even in the heat of the moment, she could be counted on. She would make a great investigator. Aerie handed her a cup of coffee, a latte, her favorite. And I dropped a basket of fries into the fryer. Comfort food. I also started to make her a breakfast sandwich, which I knew she would eventually order.

When I heard the bell ring again, I knew Dan had left. I brought out Ellie's fries and breakfast sandwich. "Here you go, girlfriend. Your favorite."

"Now that Dan's gone, I can tell you guys."

"Tell us what?"

"Well, last night, someone broke into my house and stole the copy I had of that code you gave me."

"Are you okay?" Aerie put her hand on Ellie's arm.

"Yeah, totally fine. Only now I'm thinking about setting up cameras and investing in some real home security."

"How did they know you had it? Weren't we alone in the bank when we gave that to you?" I wondered.

"Someone ran you off the road this morning?" Aerie refreshed her coffee.

"Yeah, you guys got me into something good." She smiled just before she bit into her sandwich.

"I don't know about good, maybe dangerous." Aerie put the pot back in the coffee maker.

"No, this is fun. I was able to decode some of the document before it was stolen."

I pulled out my phone. "I still have the photos."

"I knew you would."

"Why didn't you tell Dan you had copies of the evidence?" Aerie asked.

"Because I'm currently hating on him at the moment. Besides we have Ellie on the job. And she obviously knows what she's doing."

Ellie grinned at the compliment. "I'm having my boyfriend help me out."

I nodded, recognizing a blissful blush on her cheeks. It made me wonder what Tony was doing right then.

"Mira." Aerie tapped the counter with her piece of chalk.

"What?" I snapped out of my replay of Tony kissing me at the top of the Ferris wheel.

"Ellie asked if she could see the photos you took of the encrypted paper."

"Oh. Right." I reached into my back pocket and pulled out my phone. Ellie pointed to the screen.

"This is as far as I got in deciphering the code. It's in a basic skip code. Anyone could figure it out."

"What's a skip code?" Aerie and I both asked.

"It's a simple way to encode a message. It's like super basic." She chuckled.

"So, you can figure out what it says?" I asked.

"Yes." She squinted her eyes. "But I don't know what it means."

"Huh?"

"Well, the part we decoded is a list of objects with amounts next to them." She pointed to the photo on my phone. "You see here? This says phonograph and underneath it is an amount, even skip-coded the amount is plain as day. Here it would be $650."

"It's a list of items and their prices?"

"It's a secret list of items and amounts of money." Ellie grinned.

Aerie leaned back. "So, we need to find out why it's secret."

"And who would want a secret list of objects?"

"Who would break into my house for the list? And why was the guy murdered? For a list of items and prices?"

Aerie nodded. "That's the mystery."

"Well, I know who I want to talk to first. My ex. He's involved in this somehow." I showed her a picture of Alex that was still mistakenly on my phone after I blanketly deleted him from my life. "If you spot him, stall him, and text me."

"Will do."

"Thanks Ellie, we really appreciate your help with this."

"No problem. It was actually fun. Even if it was just a simple cipher. It was still a cipher." She sat back on the stool. "Hey, are you guys going to the carnival? There's this hottie with a big hammer—"

"Mira had a date with him last night."

Ellie's grin turned lascivious. "Oh, tell, tell. He sure has some biceps."

"I thought you were dating that hacker guy?"

"I am. That doesn't mean I can't look." Ellie grinned. "How was he?"

"We just kissed." I blushed. "Don't you have a job to get back to?" I pushed affectionately at her arm.

"I do. This would be much more interesting to hear about than the banking practices of the town. But I'll go." She took her to-go coffee. "Come visit me, you guys, okay?"

"Will do." We said goodbye to Ellie as she left the diner, and Darla stormed in. She waved an accusing finger at me. "You could've told me when you left this morning." She trudged across the dining room. "My visions are all messed up. But I know something bad is going down. Mira, you really need to be careful."

Messed up visions didn't sound good, especially since I was secretly using them as a watchdog.

"Sit down. I'll make you breakfast." I told her.

"And a cup of coffee. Extra-large. With oat milk if you have it." She laid her head on the counter and I walked back into the kitchen to avoid any further reprimands.

A few moments later, Aerie came back and whispered in

my ear, "She doesn't look like she's getting much sleep. Is she okay?"

"Something about a relationship but she doesn't want to talk about it with me." Only with Arnold. I shrugged. "Besides that, what were you guys doing spying on me last night?"

Aerie wrote another order on the board. "I told her you wouldn't appreciate her checking up on you during your date. But she just did it because she was worried for your safety."

"I can take care of myself." I felt like a broken record. I nodded at the order. "Who else came in?"

"That's the reason I'm back here. Your ex, Alex? He's out front, getting an earful from your sister."

Shouts came through the counter window into the kitchen. I couldn't help but smile. Darla could be an overprotective pain sometimes, but she always had my back. It almost made up for her spying on me during my date last night. I turned my head to listen and caught a few pieces of her conversation; she knew how to use a well-placed curse word, that was for sure.

I walked back out to save Alex from the excessive tongue-lashing from my sister.

He sat at a table with Darla's five-foot frame hovering over him. He tried to melt into his chair. "Look, I don't need to take this from you." He attempted to speak over her with little effect.

"You deserve worse, taking all her trust and her money. Shame on you."

"I'm outta here." He looked up at me as I stepped out from behind the counter. "I'll meet you at your house. We need to talk."

"Yeah, sure," I said automatically.

Darla stared at me without looking at Alex as he disappeared out the door. "You're going to do what he says? Have you learned nothing?"

"Huh? Oh, leave me alone. I have questions for him. He may have information about the murder. Once I find out what I want to know, I'll get to kick him out. Something I didn't get to do the first time."

"Don't give him any money." Darla climbed back on her stool and gulped her coffee.

I returned the look. "I won't give him anything. I want to know what he was doing with our murder suspect."

"Go ahead." Aerie waved. "I can hold down the diner, it's slow. Go find out what you can."

Darla looked incredulously at Aerie and then at me. I grinned. Aerie understood me. Darla, not so much. "He's a murder suspect?"

"I saw him talking with the murder suspect. He might know something." I hung up my apron. "I'll be back Aerie; I don't plan on talking to him long."

I didn't bother to get the okay from Darla since she would be mad about it no matter what I said. The diner's bells chimed behind me as I left.

11

—————

Alex sat in the old porch swing that Jay had given me, using his heel to slowly rock back and forth. I took my time walking up the slate porch steps.

"I'm not giving you any money," I told him.

"If you play your cards right, I may give you money."

I glared at him. "If anything, you should hand over all my money right now."

"Let's talk inside." He looked over his shoulder while trying to put on the airs that he was casual and laid-back. Normal Alex stuff. I couldn't believe I hadn't seen how sketchy he was while we were dating.

"What have you gotten yourself into this time?"

"Nothing. Can we go inside?" He grew edgier by the minute.

I figured there couldn't be any harm in inviting him into the house. It wasn't like I had anything worth stealing. Besides Arnold was there and I had no doubts that he would help keep Alex in line.

"Okay, come on." I pulled my house keys out of my pocket and opened the door. The summer sun lit the stained-glass squares that lined the door and painted the floor on the inside of the living room. I motioned for him to sit down on the old floral couch Aerie and I had picked up at a local yard sale. He sat but his eyes were trained on the desk.

"You found that piece of paper inside the desk, didn't you?" he said.

"How do you know?"

"I stole it from that girl at the bank." He dropped onto the couch.

"That was you? How did you know she had it?"

He shrugged. "I was told to get it, so I got it."

"Were you the one that ran her off the road?"

"Just to scare her a bit."

"You're a class-one jerk, you know that?"

"Look, I do what I need to do to get paid."

"What? Like date me and steal all my money?"

"You and I were a different situation. I apologized for that."

"Tell me what you know about the guy in the blue hat and then leave because I don't want to talk about this anymore." All these mixed emotions about our past together were floating to the surface. It was confusing and making me mad.

He sat, trying to be cool and collected, but his leg was jumpy, which meant he was still nervous, even inside the house. "Look, I got someone after me. I'm pretty sure they're after me. I could really use a place to hide out for a bit."

I stared at him. He could not possibly be asking what I think he was asking for. "You want to stay here?"

"Looks like you got lots of room." He stood up and paced the living room and peered down the hallway. "What happened down there?"

"I had a fire in the kitchen." I shook my head to clear my mind. "It's none of your business. What makes you think I'd let you stay here? After everything you did to me?"

He stood and paced the floor, edging closer to me. He reached into his back pocket and pulled out a wad of $100 bills. "Look, I can pay you."

"You mean you can give me back the money you stole."

He looked at me, beseechingly. "Yeah, okay, I guess I can do that. I owe you. But can I stay here and hide out?" He peeled off ten of those bills and handed them to me.

I wasn't proud. I snatched those bills out of his hand before he could change his mind. I eyed him critically. He had gotten in over his head with something.

"Who's to say I don't just turn you in right now for theft and endangerment or whatever for running Ellie off the road?"

"You wouldn't do that to your old lover, would you?"

"Don't nauseate me."

"Besides, you can't turn me in. You weren't supposed to have that piece of paper anyway. I know you kept a copy on your phone. Even the police don't have the original anymore." He took a moment to look clever.

"That paper was in the desk I bought, which made it mine, before it was evidence. I've done nothing wrong. You stole it from the evidence locker?"

"Nope. You wouldn't find me within a hundred miles of a police station."

"We're within a half mile of the police station right now, idiot."

"You know what I mean. I wouldn't be caught dead in there." He stuck the bills back into his pocket. "Let me stay, right?"

"Okay, but only if you pay me back everything you

stole." I was going to get my money, even if I had to live with my awful ex for a few days to get it. Plus, it would make my sister and Dan crazy, and that was totally worth it. I grinned at Alex.

He gave me a terrified look.

"You heard me. I want all the money you stole from me. You obviously have it."

"I got to live off this money. And it looks like I'm going to be on the run. I need it."

"I don't care. You want to stay here? Give me the rest of the money you owe me."

He pinched his lips and actually looked annoyed. "You're a real piece of work, you know that?"

"You are welcome to leave." I reached over and pulled open the porch door.

"You won't tell anyone I'm here? I can stay as long as I want?"

"I don't know about 'as long as you want', but for the time being, yes. Where's my money?"

He reluctantly fished in his pocket for the cash, quickly counted out ten more bills, and stuffed them in my hand.

"I think you're under-counting. Cough it up."

He pulled off five more bills and handed them to me. I looked down and saw the $2500 that he had stolen from me. I couldn't believe I had it back. I folded the bills quickly and stuffed them in my pocket. This was the best kind of closure.

"You stay a few days. That's it. I'm not feeding you and you can sleep on the couch. If I hear one footstep on the stairs, you're out of here."

"You won't let anyone know I'm here? Including that detective friend of yours?"

"No. But you should know, Darla is staying with me for the rest of the week."

The look on his face was priceless. "You're kidding me."

"Feel free to leave." I shook my head. "Sometimes you're so dumb, Alex."

He threw himself on the couch like a log.

"Take your shoes off. My couch is new."

"Don't look new."

"That's because you stole all my savings. I had to buy it used." I kicked his boot. He begrudgingly sat up, took off his boots, laid back down, and put an arm over his eyes.

"I'm going back to work. You steal anything out of this house, I will hunt you down."

"You don't have anything worth stealing anyway."

I left him to his misery, walked out the door and locked it again. I wondered for a moment how I was going to break this news to Darla. She wouldn't like it. But at least I could tell her I got my money back. I smiled the entire walk to the bank. For the moment, I ignored the fact that he hadn't given me any more information about our suspect or told me who had paid him to steal the cipher. But I could worry about that later. I finally had my money.

AFTER I RETURNED to the diner, the conversation with Darla didn't go as well as I thought it would, and I had some pretty low expectations. When I told her she could stay at the B&B down the street I could tell she was very close to taking me up on the offer.

"No, I need to keep an eye on you two."

"What for?"

"So you don't fall under his charms again and give him all the money he gave you."

"The money is already in the bank. He can't take it back.

I need it to finish the kitchen." I didn't think Darla understood how much I had changed since I got here. "He's no good and I know it, Darla. Letting him stay in the house is a small inconvenience to endure so I could get my money." I shifted on my feet. "Now, are you going to head to the B&B? I can call the woman who owns it."

"No." She put down her hands. "I'll stay, but he won't hear the end of what I have to say to him."

"I'm sure he'll be thrilled to hear that." Somehow, I was happier than I had been in months. I had gotten back what was stolen from me and I could finally close the door on my past with Alex. Plus Darla and Alex were about to hash it out in my living room. I'd pay money to see that go down. A laughed gurgled up. I couldn't help it.

"What's so funny?" Darla asked.

"Nothing. I just have a feeling Alex won't be staying that long after all." I refreshed her coffee and went back into the kitchen. It was time to prep for the lunch rush. When I walked into the refrigerator, I saw my container of cherry jam. As soon as I found time, I would start the ice cream base. It would give me something else to focus on instead of everything else going on in my crazy life.

Darla's cell phone rang. "I've got to take this." She put a twenty on the counter and left.

I HAD a batch of fries cooking in the fryer when sirens echoed outside.

Aerie stood at the windows watching police cars scream by. "They're heading up to the carnival grounds."

My first thought: I hoped nothing had happened to Tony. My second: Was this connected to the murder?

I tried to keep prepping for lunch, but all I could do was wish I had exchanged cell numbers with Tony so I could check if he was okay. All I wanted was some information about what was happening. I didn't have to wait long. Ellie came in for lunch and gave us the inside scoop. "They found a body in the haunted house. In the mirror maze."

I knew exactly where that was, and my mind imagined the body reflected over and over again in a gruesome kaleidoscope. I didn't want to ask but the words fell out of my mouth just the same. "Do they know who it was?"

"Everyone is mum over at the carnival grounds, they won't say who it is, if they know. Dan is working with the coroner."

"Who did you manage to get the info from?" I asked.

"Supposedly your sister was at the scene of the crime. Mrs. Orsa overheard her and Dan arguing. Your sister is a suspect."

"What?" I hadn't seen Darla after our conversation, when she took the phone call. I had assumed she went home to have it out with Alex. I glanced at Aerie.

"Go." She waved at me. "I can handle the rest of lunch. Find out what's going on."

I hung up my apron and walked out the front door toward the police station. I had to know what my sister had been doing at a murder scene.

12

I power-walked my way down to the station. I pushed the doors open and saw Darla sitting across from Dan in the conference room. She waved her arms around to explain something, like she always did. At least she wasn't handcuffed. Back in Massachusetts, Darla showed up at a number of murder scenes before the police realized she wasn't a suspect and subsequently learned she was a psychic. Dan followed the rules by the book though, and I watched as he got an earful from Darla. She was obviously telling him how it was.

The officer at the front desk knew me, but she wasn't happy about letting me go back to talk to Dan until she noticed he was getting berated by Darla.

"I think I can help with that." I pointed.

She reluctantly nodded and I took a second to relish Darla having a field day on Dan. I pushed open the door.

"You don't understand, there were two people. One with muscles, one with the gun."

"This is all hearsay. You don't know this for fact."

"I'm a psychic, Detective Lockheart. With my amount of experience, I know when it's true, and this is true."

"Hi guys," I announced. Both of them stopped mid-breath, ready to launch into another argument with each other.

"I'm hearing around town, you're the most likely suspect?" I half laughed as I told Darla.

"Where did you hear that from?" Dan asked, obviously concerned that word was spreading fast.

"You know how the rumor mill runs in this town, Detective Lockheart."

"Your sister is free to go, Mira. She just doesn't want to leave. It must run in the family. Is there a gene for discovering murder victims?"

"Yes. It's called psychic ability," Darla said.

"Whoa." I put up my hands. "Don't imply that I have the Gift. That's just you."

She ignored my protest and turned back to Dan. "I'm telling you, you need to be looking for two suspects. Not just one."

"I'll keep that under advisement."

Darla turned to me while pointing at Dan. "Is he always this frustrating?"

"You have no idea." I took Darla by the arm and escorted her out of the conference room. "Come on, let's go. I can feed you some lunch."

We turned our backs on the fuming Dan Lockheart and left the police station.

"Do they know who was killed?" I asked Darla, hoping she had gotten some information out of Dan.

"The guy in the blue hat. Or who we may assume is the guy we've seen with the blue hat."

Relief flooded my body. Tony was okay, then. "Why were you at the murder scene?"

"I told you, my visions have been really messed up since I got here. But after you and I talked I got a very clear one about the hall of mirrors at the carnival."

"And?"

"As soon as I got the vision, I went to the carnival to see if I could find the location. Like I said, my visions have been inconsistent and I wasn't sure if this was a vision I could trust. So, I wanted to check it out."

"Why did Dan think you were a suspect?"

"Because the carnival wasn't open yet, and I was the one to discover the body. The death was by gunshot wound, and I don't have powder residue on my hands. So, I'm no longer suspect, you'll be thankful to know."

"It's okay. Dan suspected me in at least two murders."

"What kind of town do you live in?"

"I could ask the same of you." I nudged her with my elbow.

Darla nodded sagely. "I suppose you and I are both drawn to places that need our skills.

My heart sank. Sure, I could talk to my cat and see my house-ghost. But that was it. My skills were definitely not Darla's skills. Still, I had legitimately solved crimes in this town. I should be proud of that. Except that I couldn't help but compare myself to my sister. "I think we need to have a talk with Alex."

"I can't believe you have him living in your house. What if he had a hand in this murder?"

"He's definitely involved with something shady. But he's not calling the shots—someone is paying him to get rid of evidence. We need to find out who that is. After that, we'll send him on his way."

Darla made a curt nod and we walked together back to the house.

A TRAIL of trash led from the living room to the kitchen area. "What is this?" I had just swept the floors.

Arnold answered for me. *Your friend is not the neatest of eaters. He also gave me treats to shut me up. But my alliance is with you; therefore, I'm letting you know I believe he ate all of your special potato chips.*

"Alex! What is this? You're in my house for like an hour tops and create this kind of mess?"

"I'm hungry. You didn't feed me at the diner."

He did eat all of my chips. The empty bag lay crushed up on the couch. "You ate all of them Alex, all of them. Do you know how far away the supermarket is here?"

"Did you bring back any food?"

"No, but you and I need to have a serious conversation about your friend with the hat."

"Ray is not my friend. I just work with him at the carnival."

"Past tense. He's dead. Murdered."

Alex's eyes grew wide. "You have to protect me!" He grabbed my arm. I yanked it away. He stared beseechingly at my sister. "Darla, you have some of those crazy witchy skills, right?"

If I were a psychic, which I'm not, I would bet that Darla's aura was turning a bright angry red at Alex's reference of "witchy skills." Darla hated when people used witch as a flippant adjective like that. Especially Alex. In my mind's eye, I imagined her throttling him until he turned blue in the face. But in reality she stormed off into the other room and I was left alone with Alex.

"Your buddy received a low caliber gunshot wound to the chest. That could've been you, couldn't it?" I glared at him. "Or maybe you shot him and then showed up at the diner?"

"I need to get the heck out of here. But then they'd find me and kill me."

"You need to tell me what's going on. And tell me who paid you to get rid of the cipher."

"What do you mean?"

"Really? You're going to play it this way?" I walked down the hall to my front door and opened it. "You're welcome to leave."

Alex came up around me and pushed the door closed. "Look, you keep me here without letting anyone know and I'll tell you what's going on."

"Now we're getting somewhere." I sat down at the folding table in the dining room and motioned for Alex to sit. "Spill it."

Taco let out a huge squawk that made Alex jump out of his skin. I couldn't help but giggle. "It's just my bird, relax."

Alex glared at Taco who squawked again, "Sexy girls, sexy girls. Raaah!"

"Where'd you pick up that red feathered drama?"

"None of your business. Now tell me."

"Look, I'm not going to lie, working at the carnival was pretty good. The pay sucked but there were lots of girls." He had the nerve to wink. But when I gave him a stern look, he cleared his throat. "There was also a couple of us guys who liked to skim off the top."

"What do you mean by 'skim'?"

"You know, take a little bit of the money from the ticket booth."

"Why am I not surprised you're stealing money from somebody?"

"Look, a guy's got to get by."

I shook my head. Alex would never learn. This was who he was. "So, tell me about the guy in the blue hat."

"Ray. Man, I can't believe he's dead. Actually, I can. Once Joel bought it, we knew we were next."

"Do you know who killed them?"

"Obviously somebody who owns the carnival, or their muscle."

"Do you know who that would happen to be?" A picture of Tony leaning in to kiss me flashed into my mind. I shook my head.

"No, but obviously they want their money back."

"How much did you steal?"

"Ten grand."

"I'm glad I got my money before you get bumped off."

"Don't say that." He looked around nervously. "You're gonna jinx me."

Taco squawked again making Alex twitch and go pale.

"Did it ever occur to you that maybe you shouldn't have stolen the money in the first place?" I stood up. "You never learn, Alex."

"You and Darla will help me, right?"

"Alex, you brought this on yourself. But I personally need to find out who the killer is."

I didn't tell him I needed to make sure that the new guy I started dating wasn't also a criminal. Maybe it was me that never learned.

"Yeah, yeah, Alex. I'm going to try to figure out who the

murderer is. But this doesn't get you off the hook. Most likely you'll still get arrested."

He looked like he had swallowed raw fish. "I guess that's better than being dead."

"Yeah, I suppose jail is better than being dead." I walked down the hallway. "Darla, let's go get some lunch. We need to talk."

I was also okay with leaving Alex to stew in his own juices for a while. Maybe he'll finally realize crime doesn't pay. Although it did make me wonder where he was keeping that ten grand he said he stole. Most likely he'd stolen more than that. If I knew Alex, he wouldn't share with me the full amount for fear I would ask for it. He was dumb but he wasn't stupid.

13

I grabbed Darla and we walked back to the diner. "You do realize that this means Alex is a prime suspect? Why on earth did you ever date him?"

I wasn't about to tell her that it was because she told me not to. "You never fell for a hot guy just because?" She shrugged. I added, "Hotness aside, Alex couldn't kill anybody, he's not competent enough."

"I won't disagree with you there. But your friend Dan Lockheart will want him for questioning."

"I'm still mad at you for telling him to watch over me. I don't think I've forgiven you yet."

"So, you're not going to talk to Detective Lockheart?"

"No. You're lucky I'm talking to you."

"I should be able to solve this little mystery."

"My town. My mystery. My ex-boyfriend is involved. My no-longer-potential-boyfriend is involved. My mystery."

Darla put up her hands. "My visions have been all screwed up lately. But I don't think you should be searching for a murderer."

I stood stock still on the sidewalk. And I gaped at her. "You do it all the time."

"But I'm psychic."

"And there it is. I'm not a psychic so I'm not good enough."

"That's not what I said. What I mean is my psychic skills keep me safe. You don't have psychic skills so..."

"So, I'm crap."

"That's not what I'm saying..."

I pushed open the door to the diner and stormed my way back to the kitchen. Aerie watched me fly past. Then she noticed Darla. "Are you guys not talking again?"

"No!" I shouted.

"Sibling love. I know it all too well." Aerie chuckled. "What can I get you for lunch, Darla?"

"If Mira promises not to spit in my meal, I'd love a falafel because the last time she made one, it was really good." She shouted that last part into the kitchen. Trying to butter me up. Well, it wouldn't work. I was still extremely mad at her and she just reinforced the whole issue by bringing up being psychic.

I looked up at the order board. Nothing for me to prep, except Darla's falafel. With a huge sigh, I settled into making her lunch. This argument between us was nothing new. I reminded myself she'd be heading home soon, and I would have my life back.

When I finished, I placed the falafel plate on the counter and glanced out at Darla using her cell phone to manage the career of being a famous in-demand psychic.

I needed a pick-me-up. It was time to make the cherry almond ice cream.

I started by taking all the ingredients I'd need out of the refrigerator. The milk would have to be heated to dissolve the sugar. I would use Mr. Miller's fresh eggs for the custard, too. As I slowly, methodically, laid out everything on the counter, I calmed down enough to think again. The one glaring thing that screamed in my mind was Tony. Did he do this? He got really upset when I mentioned that the man in the blue hat broke into my house. His words echoed in my head: "I'll take care of it." He had so quickly switched back to his easy happy demeanor that I hadn't thought anything of it at the time. But now? And with Darla and her psychic mumbo jumbo, which I knew wasn't mumbo jumbo, telling me not to trust any man I met this week.

I put the milk and eggs back into the refrigerator, the cherry jam too. I had to find out for myself.

"Aerie, I need to leave, I'm really sorry."

She cornered me in the kitchen. "What is this about?"

"I have to make sure Tony didn't do this."

"You think he did?"

"I just have alarm bells going off in my head and I need to find out what they mean."

She grabbed my forearm. "Be careful."

I nodded.

I hung up my apron and made a beeline for the door, ignoring the inquisitions from my sister as the diner door fell closed behind me.

14

Just outside the diner, I had my head down, thinking of how to figure out if Tony was innocent or not. If I had him take me to the crime scene, maybe I could read his face. Because if I asked, I'm sure he'd insist he was innocent. Not paying attention at all, I ran squarely into someone. He caught me by the shoulders before I could trip. "Whoa." He set me on my feet.

"Tony." I looked up into his face. "I was just...why are you here?"

"I wanted to make sure you were okay."

"Yeah, I'm fine."

"There was a murder. It was Ray, and after you told me about him breaking into your house, I just felt I needed to check on you, make sure you were okay." His hands brushed my arms lightly as he let go.

"I'm fine. I was actually coming up to see you."

The right corner of his mouth turned up. "You were?"

I nodded. My plan to read Tony's face at the murder site disappeared. Or had it? "Can we walk?"

"Sure." He gave me a confused look but walked with me just the same, back the way he had come, toward the carnival grounds. "Are you sure you're okay?" he asked.

I was going to have to make something up. "It's just shocking to hear of two murders in the same week while the carnival is in town."

He nodded knowingly. "We're packing it up tomorrow morning. Tonight will be our last night here." He paused for a moment. "Where are we walking?"

With the carnival leaving town early, all the possible murder suspects connected to the carnival, would leave. And, as new as my feelings were, I liked Tony. He was such a sweet guy. Of course, contingent on him not being a murderer.

"Can we walk back to the carnival?"

"Why? I mean sure, but why now when the police are still cleaning...everything?"

Should I tell him that I help solve crimes for the town? Would that keep him from sharing information with me? I came up with an idea to divert this. "Okay, so the scariest place in town right now is the carnival because of the murder, and I believe in getting back on the horse when you fall off."

"So, you get over your fear."

That worked. "Yes. Can we?"

"I'll go with you, sure." He tensed up a bit. But he walked along side me without saying a word.

"Do you know when it happened?"

"Sometime late last night. After we closed for the night. Around eleven. We all heard the shot, but thought it was someone setting off a firework."

"He was shot?"

"It happened in the haunted house in the room with the mirrors."

Even though I already knew of that, hearing it from Tony made me sad. The happy memory of thousands of reflections of Tony and me was now tarnished. "That's too bad."

"Yeah," he agreed.

We continued in silence for most of the walk to the grounds.

"Are you sure you want to do this?" Tony asked.

"I can't not do it. I have to see what happened." I needed to know if he did it. If we arrived at the scene of the crime together, I could watch for his reaction, if there was one. My own self-confidence was at stake here. I needed to know if it was true that I keep choosing the wrong kinds of men.

The scene was an ordered chaos. It appeared that the entire police force was standing outside the haunted house. The coroner had pulled their vehicle onto the grass within a few hundred feet of the scene.

Tony took my hand and squeezed it gently.

I had to get closer if I wanted to see anything.

"Are you okay?"

I winced. "Yes, I'm fine. I just...can we get a little closer?"

"Closer?"

"It's just that it looks the same as it always does...well, except there's a coroner parked out front."

"If you need to get closer to it all, I'll come with you."

Was he being protective and supportive, or making sure I didn't see anything that would incriminate him?

We walked closer to the structure. I tried to peer over one of the police officers' shoulders. I couldn't see much but then there was a shuffling at the entrance as they brought the body out. The dark black body bag was completely closed. I couldn't make out any more than that and the gurney.

Tony squeezed my hand. I wasn't sure if it was for my reassurance or his. I watched his face closely. He looked pained. Not angry, not defiant, but again I questioned my ability to gauge the men I dated.

When the coroner closed the vehicle door, Tony turned to me, and our eyes met. "You're really brave, you know that?"

I brushed off the compliment. "No, I'm not." My cheeks felt hot. I never took compliments well.

"You are, and I'm really proud to know you. He leaned down enough to give me a reassuring hug that was generous and warm. I took a moment to simply be. This hug felt genuine, so why couldn't I get the word "suspect" out my mind? I looked over his shoulder and saw Dan stare directly at us as he exited the haunted house. The hug ended clumsily.

"I think we should go." No need to have an awkward conversation with Dan in front of Tony.

Tony grinned and held my hand. His phone buzzed and he didn't release my hand to check the text. But he did angle the phone away from me so I couldn't read it. "Looks like I have to work right now. But promise, you'll come see me later? To say goodbye?"

"Sure." The sooner I got out of here the better. I watched Dan head toward a police cruiser and disappear inside. I smiled at Tony. "I'll come by after dinner."

Tony held my hand all the way to the edge of the carnival grounds. "I'll see you later."

I stepped out onto the sidewalk.

"Hey, Mira?"

"Yeah?"

He turned, looked at me like he wanted to say something more, but then just waved goodbye. "Oh, nothing. I'll see you later."

"Okay." I walked down the street wondering what he wanted to ask me.

I had a pressing need to use the bathroom, and it wasn't like I could turn back to use the carnival's porta-potties so, I raced home. As soon as I entered the house, I knew something was up. Arnold purred around my ankles and Ozzy yipped to go for a walk, all perfectly normal things. Arnold queued me in on the discrepancy.

The double-crosser left. He gave me a pile of treats and fed Ozzy human food to keep us busy while he snuck out.

The house was silent. Alex was gone? Instantly I was angry. I didn't get to kick him out. For the second time, he denied me. "Ooh, that creep. Good riddance."

I walked Ozzy quickly out front and hoped whatever Alex fed her would be okay for her digestion and I wouldn't have a clean-up mission later this afternoon. Then I realized what time it was.

Aerie had to close up without my help. I sighed. Putting Ozzy back in the house, I petted Arnold and told him to stand guard. Alex wasn't welcome back.

Understood. He flexed his not-so-unremarkable claws.

I WALKED across the street directly to Aerie's house.

Once inside her cozy kitchen I apologized. "I'm sorry for not getting back in time to help with close up."

"It's totally fine. It was quiet. No worries. Are you okay?"

"I'm fine, but I'm really sorry you had to close up by yourself."

"I was more worried about you. Did you ask Tony if he...?"

"Not outright. But I had him take me to the murder scene."

She gave me a concerned look. "And?"

"He didn't look guilty. I don't think he did it."

"You don't sound so sure."

"No, I'm sure. He just couldn't do something like that."

"He looks like he could."

I didn't argue. Tony's physique was intimidating. But his personality was sweet and kind and thoughtful. However, I thought Alex was fine when we started dating too, and that turned out horribly. Was my radar about guys always off? For some reason, this seemed like more of a pressing question than who was running around murdering people.

"I don't know what to do," I said.

"Don't go out with him."

"The carnival is only in town another night. How much trouble can I get into going out with Tony again? And I already promised him I'd see him tonight."

"Even Darla doesn't want you to do it."

"Darla never wants me to date anyone."

"Look maybe we can figure this whole thing out without you going to the extreme of dating a killer."

"He's not a killer."

"Are you sure?"

I nodded.

"Are you sure enough to bet your life on it?"

I didn't nod this time. "Per the rules, everyone stays a suspect until they are not."

"At which point we've solved who the murderer is."

"Come on." I stood up. "Let's practice throwing darts. You can see Sam, and we can hash this all out over a slice of pizza."

"Fine by me. I'll bring some paper and a pen. We can write everything down."

AERIE CALLED Sam to let him know that we were coming. So, when we opened the front doors to the Pizza Pub, our pies were waiting for us.

She giggled and ran to Sam and gave him a big smooch on the cheek. "Hey, honey, how's it going?"

"Better now that you're here," he said with a smile.

Gary Balinsky waited at the counter while Sam put together his Italian sub. The guy loved this place. We exchanged an awkward greeting. I was the one who found out he had been poisoned and by whom: someone close enough to Gary that I felt badly. I decided it was best if I took my pizza and sat in a booth closest to the dartboard. I needed to blow off some steam, and ever since we'd tried the dart balloon game at the carnival, I was itching to practice again. I took a quick glance over at the empty corner stage. Aerie had talked me into a karaoke night not too long ago, which had resulted in a bar brawl. My luck wasn't all that great; trouble followed me wherever I went. But this was the first time I had feelings for someone who might be a killer.

"What's with that look on your face?" Aerie sat down with her pizza. "If you're thinking about Tony, you do realize he has to be on the suspect list, right?"

"I know. I need to figure this out. He can't have done it." I took a bite of Sam's delicious pizza. Already I felt a bit better. Comfort food works wonders. "Let's create our suspect list."

"Let me eat first." She laughed, grabbed a slice and tore off a mouthful. Even though her mouth was full, she managed to get out, "Here's the pen and paper. You start."

I stared down at the blank piece of paper and wrote Tony's name at the top. I took a deep breath and bit into my slice of pizza. "We also know that most of the carnival workers could also be on this list." I looked up at Aerie to see if she agreed. She nodded. "Yeah, but Tony owns the place and he's a big guy. Your sister said someone with muscles and someone with a gun."

"Lots of guys have muscles and aren't killers."

"Okay, okay. Let's talk about the other suspects."

"Alex is definitely going on this list too. I saw him running around with the second victim. The guy with the hat, Ray?"

"Did he tell you anything about what he was doing with him?"

"Someone ordered him to steal back the list and he managed to grab it from Ellie."

"Okay, so Alex is on the list. Did he happen to mention anything else? Like who asked him to steal the list?"

"He was too afraid to tell me. At the time he thought he would be the next victim. I told him he could stay at the house but when I got back, he was gone."

"That's kind of suspicious behavior."

"Alex is always suspicious."

Aerie raised an eyebrow, obviously questioning my decision-making skills if I had already known he was suspicious.

"I'm an idiot for guys with a cute smile?"

Instead of commenting, Aerie laughed, shook her head, and filled her mouth with more pizza.

"The only real clue we have is that cipher. Which Ellie says is just a list of household stuff with prices next to it."

"But big prices." Aerie pointed her pizza slice at me.

"Yeah. So, somebody is selling stuff for big money, and our second victim had a list of them."

"We really don't have a lot of clues."

"No. We don't. But I have an idea of how we can get more."

"Am I going to regret this?"

"Probably."

"I'm in. But after I finish my pizza." Aerie exchanged a loving glance with Sam. She deserved some time with her boyfriend, even if it was just watching him sling pizza dough behind the counter.

"And after I throw some darts and imagine Alex's face. At least I got back the money he stole from me." I explained that whole ordeal to Aerie, wondering again, why my jerk-radar didn't work when it came to relationships.

I took a couple huge bites of another slice of pizza, got up, and grabbed the darts off the board. I stood across from the booth next to Aerie and tossed them at the dartboard using the skills we learned at the balloon-popping booth at the carnival. I was consistently hitting closer to the bullseye.

"You know? I feel like we should go back to the carnival and win some mice and talk to that woman who taught us how to throw darts. Jessie, was that her name? For some reason, I think she's involved."

"Maybe she would have information about the carnival that Tony wasn't willing to share," Aerie added.

"It's only four o'clock. Still early yet, so it shouldn't be too busy." Aerie finished up her pizza. "Do you have a stack of dollar bills you don't mind sacrificing at the dart booth?"

"I'm going to win every single animal she has, live or stuffed." I threw a dart and it hit the center of the board, then fell on the floor. "At the very least I'll get some information."

15

______

We left the Pizza Pub and drove to the high school, parking next to the flea market. We planned on walking to the carnival. But seeing empty tables and tents, I had an idea. The flea market wouldn't start up again until the weekend, and while the airstream was still marked with police tape, the whole place was deserted. The perfect opportunity to check for clues at our own pace. We had been so hurried the first time. But now there was no danger of Dan showing up and arresting me for breaking and entering into a crime scene. Aerie and I quietly crouched in the grass, planning our approach to the mobile home. We snuck over from opposite sides of the trailer to make sure no one was nearby. As I came around the back, I accidentally stubbed my toes on a rock that was behind the back tire. "Ouch."

"Shh." Aerie put her finger to her lips as we got closer to the door. I pantomimed that I would walk in if she opened the door. She nodded. Once the door was open, it was important for us to get inside as quickly as possible and close the door behind us. It would take a bit for our eyes to adjust to the dark but that's what the flashlight setting on our phone was for.

I crept closer to the door. Aerie reached up and yanked it open. I charged into the dark interior of the trailer and Aerie swept in behind me closing the door with a thud.

I reached out my arms in the dark and hit something soft. Nope, *someone* large and right in front of me. I screamed and so did the person. I turned around and bumped into Aerie when I recognized the sound of the responding scream. "Alex?"

"Mira? What are you doing here?" He flipped on a lantern near the door.

Aerie squeezed next to me.

My eyes adjusted to the dim light. "I could ask you the same thing. Why are you hiding out here?"

"You didn't tell me your house was haunted! Between someone, a ghost or something, singing in my ear all the time, and your sister harassing me, I couldn't stand it. I'd rather take my chances with the cops." His voice rang with fear.

"You realize this trailer is still police evidence? They could come by at any time."

"I'm betting the person who wants to kill me is less likely to show up at one of their own crime scenes."

I glanced around the small space. It hadn't changed much from when I saw it last: old, worn, and smelly. The same antiques magazine lay on the table, the sink had dirty cups and a plate; there wasn't much else to see.

"Spill it, Alex. What is going on? Tell us what you know and we won't tell the police we saw you here."

He backed up and sat on the bench along the wall. "It wasn't supposed to go down like this. We were just trying to skim."

"From the carnival?"

"Right. But Joel got this idea that we could make even more money if we could blackmail... Well, I can't tell you. They'd kill me for sure."

"Tony?"

"You're better not knowing. I just want to ride this out, and go in the opposite direction when the carnival leaves tonight. This racket was jinxed from the beginning." He shook his head. "Look, it was supposed to be easy. They steal stuff and then sell it. It's like a whole black-market thing."

"At the flea market?"

"Yeah. And Joel and I wanted in on it. Ray kept trying to talk us out of it; he knew we were getting into something too dangerous." Alex put up his hands and rubbed his face. "I'm gonna catch it next. There's a bullet with my name on it. It's just waiting for me."

"Not if we can figure this out, Alex. We can put them in jail, and you can..." I realized he would more than likely end up in jail, too. At least he wouldn't be dead.

"So, what did you guys do?"

"We stole a list. I couldn't tell you who had created it, who's murdering people. Actually, Joel created a copy in his secret code he liked to brag about." He shifted in his seat. "Once we had it, we knew we could link the thefts to the carnival if we went to the cops, so we sent anonymous notes to the carnival manager's office. To blackmail them. It should have been easy."

"And?"

"And nothin'. A few days later, we found Joel outside here, dead, worm-food." He stood and paced the tiny area. "That's when I saw you in town." His pacing became more frantic. "I swear I'm done with grifting this time."

"I bet you say that every time."

"This time I mean it." His eyes met mine and I could see the fear in them.

I reached out and took his arm. "We can figure this out, Alex. I can have Dan put them in jail and you'll be safe."

He ran his hand through his hair. "Sorry if I don't feel as confident as you. If this detective friend of yours goes after them, and they think I ratted them out, well... Just swear you won't tell anybody I'm here." He glanced at Aerie who shook her head.

"We won't." I turned to go. "We'll find them, Alex. Promise." Of course, it would be easier if he would just tell us who *they* were. I didn't know if he really didn't know or if he was too afraid to tell us. I honestly couldn't blame him. He didn't know our track record for catching murderers.

Once we were outside again, I took a deep cool breath. I promised Alex because I needed to prove it wasn't Tony. But what if it was?

"You can't go on another date with Tony."

"I have to."

"Listen. No, you don't. We can solve this some other way."

"My luck with guys has never been good, obviously. I have to know one way or the other. I have to find out for myself."

"Promise me you'll be careful?"

"I'll have my cell phone and I'll call you if anything happens. I need to get ready."

I DECIDED to go a little more casual than the sundress. If I had to sneak around anywhere, I didn't want to be hampered by my dress. I wore a stretchy skort: a spandex skirt with shorts underneath, and a sleeveless blouse I picked up at the big box store. The only catch was that I didn't have a pocket to put my cell phone. Once ready, I headed downstairs to the dining room to go over the plan with Aerie and Darla.

Aerie brought me a wristlet to borrow. Which was pretty much a wallet that could hold my phone. A strap attached to the side let me carry it discretely. "The purse will have to do."

"You look nice."

I glanced at my sister and Aerie as they sat at the table. They both looked worried.

"It's going to be fine. In and out. I just need to learn if Tony did this thing, and if I can find evidence to clear him, all the better. I'll be out of there before you guys even realize it."

"Going on this date goes against every intuitive bone in my body," Darla announced. "I really don't like it."

"I've done it before."

"Well..." Aerie tipped her head. "You've never dated a potential murderer before."

"I don't think he did it."

"He's still a suspect. Please be careful." Aerie closed the zipper on the wristlet for me.

"I've got my phone. I'll text you if I need something." I took a deep breath. "Hold down the fort, guys. I'll see you in a little bit." Just before I left, Arnold rubbed my shin.

Want me to come along? I have the claws.

I reached down and petted him on the head. "I'll be alright, buddy. Be back in a few." I walked out the door and began the trek up the street to my date with, I had to remember, a suspect. My palms were already sweating.

ONCE I SAW HIM, I relaxed. Tony was busy helping to fix a tent pole on the goldfish booth. He looked up and noticed me. The smile on his face was so honest. He just couldn't be a killer. But I checked myself; my jerk-meter was off. I had such rotten luck with men for so long, how would I know if I met someone decent? I smiled back. "Hey there." I jogged up the slope. Tony met me halfway. "I'm glad you came. You seemed a little spooked when I took you to the crime scene, so I wasn't sure."

I wasn't about to tell him this was a common occurrence where I was concerned. Or that I was more disconcerted by watching the guy I wasn't dating witness me holding hands with the guy I was dating. It was complicated. "I'm fine."

"I have to stick close by, because of everything." He pointed to a walkie-talkie clipped to his hip. "But would you be up for a quiet stroll?"

"Sure." I followed his lead. We walked to the edge of the carnival grounds closer to the high school. We sauntered along the perimeter of the carnival. "Thanks for agreeing to see me again." Tony's demeanor seemed forlorn.

"I had fun the other night." I still hadn't forgotten the kiss at the top of the Ferris wheel.

He nodded and smiled. "Yeah, me too." He offered me his hand.

I hesitated a second, but only a second, and then took it. His grip was warm and firm and comforting. And yet, a shiver went down my spine. Tony had to remain a suspect until we found the killer. I had to keep that in mind. But right now, here we were safely in public and if I had to, I could run into the crowd and get lost. But I didn't feel like I would have to. "Tony, do you know who might have killed those men?"

He squeezed my hand slightly and was silent for a long moment. "It has to be somebody that works at the carnival."

I nodded. "I thought so, too."

"I just don't know who would do such a thing." He turned to me slightly. "I mean, I know these people. I don't understand."

"Did you know that Ray and Joel were stealing money from the carnival?"

"What?" There was no mistaking the shock in his voice. "I don't handle the financials. I manage the staff and the equipment." He stopped walking and turned to me, letting go of my hand. "Wait, how do you know those two were skimming off the profits?"

I cringed. I really couldn't tell him about Alex. Especially not if Tony was still a suspect. That would be like signing Alex's death warrant. I mulled that over for a second. No. I couldn't do it. "I was just asking around and found out."

"I guess it just goes to show, sometimes you just don't know people." He reached out and took my hand again. "It just makes me sad."

This time I gripped his hand reassuringly. We walked around the edges of the carnival. He suddenly stopped. "I totally forgot, I have something for you."

"For me?"

The smile he gave me made me forget about everything else. "Come with me?"

I nodded. I followed him as he made a right towards the flea market grounds where the trailers were parked. I had to jog to keep up with him. He was as excited as a school kid on the last day of school. A couple yards ahead of me he opened the door to an RV. He waved me over. "Come on in."

I made it up the two steps into the RV, and when the door slammed shut behind me, an ominous foreboding made my stomach sink. Was I now trapped inside an RV with the killer? The grin on my face wavered. As if he knew what I was thinking, he took my hand. "Don't worry, we won't stay long. Sit here." He motioned to the seat next to the table. I'll be right back." He disappeared into the back, which I assumed was the bedroom.

My stomach was a mess of butterflies. Should I duck out the door now while he was occupied? But within seconds the door opened and he came out carrying something I couldn't see. As he came closer, my muscles tightened and then I realized he held a delicate necklace.

"This is for you." He draped the necklace over my palm.

"It's the evil eye. It's supposed to protect you from evil." He shrugged. "It's all superstition and everything but it's kind of a big deal among our group."

"Thank you." The necklace was a beautiful glass bead in white and blue. I unfastened it, but my hands were shaking too much to handle the clasp.

"Here, let me." Tony's large but dexterous fingers took hold of the tiny ends and fastened it quickly around my neck. "It looks beautiful on you."

"You didn't have to get me anything."

"Like I said, I really enjoyed seeing you the other night, and I wanted to give you something to remember me by. Especially since we're leaving tomorrow."

"It's lovely."

"Maybe you'll remember me? And we can have a date again next summer?"

Words wouldn't come. I simply nodded.

"Come on, let's get out of the stuffy room. And finish our walk."

Tony stood and headed for the door. As I followed him out, I noticed an item that was oddly placed in this state-of-the-art RV. An antique phonograph sat in the corner behind the driver's seat. My mind flashed back to the decoded list that Ellie had cracked for us. Phonograph: $650.

I walked down the steps and out of the RV. Tony closed the door and locked it. He took my hand, which was now sweaty with nerves. We continued our walk around the remainder of the carnival. Both of us were silent, although Tony occasionally mentioned how pretty the town was, or pointed out something of interest around us. I couldn't focus on his words. I just nodded and kept wondering why he would have a phonograph in his RV.

As soon as I could gracefully bow out of the date, I thanked Tony again for the necklace. He bent down and kissed my cheek. "You're the one bright spot in this week."

I walked home. I kept asking myself if Tony was as sweet as he seemed or if he was a really good liar. Because I couldn't sort out how he could be innocent with that phonograph in his possession. The verdict was clear. I certainly couldn't trust my own instincts anymore.

16

———

Back at home, I sat and let my forehead fall to the card table.

"But it was in his RV. If he's not the killer, which I personally think he is, he's definitely involved," Darla reminded me.

I rolled my head to the side. "I know. But he just doesn't give off the vibe of a killer."

"You've never been a very good judge of character, Mira," Darla reprimanded.

"Thanks a lot, sis. Like I don't already know that." I pushed myself up off of the table. I didn't like where this conversation was going. Namely down the road of my complete and utter lack of discernment in the character of the men I date.

"We don't know who he's working with. Darla, you did say that there were two people in your vision of Ray's death?" Aerie stood and paced.

Darla nodded. "Even though my visions have been inconsistent lately, I definitely felt two people there."

Even if Darla's visions were as messed up as she kept saying, I wouldn't dispute this one. "If there are other people involved, then we need to narrow down who those suspects could be."

"It could be anybody who works at the carnival. Everybody is directly tied to Tony because he runs the place, right?"

"Tonight is the last night of the carnival. If we are going to find out who the killer is, then we need to find out now." Darla stood.

"They'll be packing everything up tomorrow morning early," I added.

"Is everyone up for another evening at the carnival?" Darla asked.

"Let's go." Aerie headed for the door.

Part of me wanted to crawl into bed and forget about all of this, but another part of me screamed that even after what I saw, Tony was innocent.

Guilty or innocent, I had to find out, and quickly before the carnival packed up and left town.

EARLIER, we had intended to talk to the woman at the dart booth, which we hadn't done because we had been so startled seeing Alex in the airstream. My number one plan was to ask her a few questions and get her to talk.

"Back again?" The dart-booth attendant, Jessie, was already handing the darts over to me, which I took.

"I thought I'd try my luck again." I set down the darts, I took out the five-dollar bill and handed it to her. She stuffed it in the pocket of her apron. I squared my legs, pulled back my arm, took aim, and let the dart fly. The practice I had at Sam's must've helped. I popped the yellow balloon on the first try. Aerie clapped.

Jessie waved her muscular arms theatrically. "Great job. If you get all three, you get the big prize."

I threw the next dart. It stuck cleanly next to the green balloon that I had aimed for.

"Oh, too bad. You know what. I'm going to give you another dart free of charge." She handed me another dart and I took it. "There you go. Because I bet you can hit three balloons today."

"Thanks. I've got a question I'm hoping you can answer." I watched her face closely. "Do you know anything about Ray's death?"

Her open, jolly, sell-you-anything-face closed down immediately. "Nope, not a thing."

I threw a dart and popped the red balloon. She said nothing after the sound of the balloon exploded. I could tell by her demeanor she knew something. "Are you sure you don't know anything?"

She pinched her lips tight. "Lady, you gonna throw that last dart or what?"

I tossed the last dart and it hit the frame around the balloons. I didn't care. I'd gotten the information I needed. I watched her for a moment as she pulled the darts out of the board. Stuffed in her back pocket was a blue baseball cap.

I turned around quickly and hustled Darla and Aerie away from the dart booth.

"Let's get some lemonade." I announced.

"What's up with you?"

"Didn't you hear her? She absolutely knows something about the murder, if she didn't do it herself."

Darla gave me a disapproving look. "I think you're using wishful thinking. Just because you don't want it to be Tony."

"I think you're being sexist. Who says this woman couldn't be the killer?" I asked her.

"I'm not saying she couldn't be the killer; I'm just saying more evidence points towards Tony, than this woman," Darla said.

"Maybe you're right." The best way to get rid of Darla was to agree with her. If I argued, she'd stay here. And I wanted a chance to get back and grill Jessie for more information. Sometimes it worked to poke the bear.

"It's the last night of the carnival. Let's ride some rides."

This might be the easiest way to get Darla and Aerie out of my hair for a little bit.

"The view of the town from the top of the Ferris wheel is pretty fantastic. And we can ask Jim questions afterward." We only had to stand in line for a minute or two before Jim waved us up.

"Only two per seat, rules," he said.

Before they could say anything, I pushed Aerie and Darla together and they plunked down into the seat. Jim locked the metal bar across their laps and went back to the controls to move the Ferris wheel one more seat forward. Darla and Aerie would assume that I would get in the next available chair. But that was not my plan. I was going back to talk to Jessie.

"Hey, Jim, my friends really want to see the view from the top of the Ferris wheel. Can you keep them up there for a little bit?"

"Will do." He tipped the rim of his cap at me.

"Thanks, Jim." I walked back towards the dart booth. I could hear Darla shouting my name. But I ignored her, which wasn't anything new.

I stood back and watched Jessie call more people into playing darts at her booth. When she saw me out of the corner of her eye, her happy-go-lucky grin faltered but she managed to plaster it back on and continue with her schtick.

As I approached the booth, she began to pack things up. "Leaving so soon?"

"There was a murder yesterday, chickie. We are all bugging out of here tomorrow morning."

I plunked a ten on the counter. "I'd like to play."

Jessie eyed the money and me and handed over six darts. She continued to pack things up while I threw them. The first one hit nothing at all—veered off the side of the corkboard. I was glad nobody was standing close. *Focus, Mira.*

I aimed the next dart better and just nearly missed a balloon. It swayed back and forth in the breeze of the shot. "You have a great view of the flea market from here, don't you?"

The words my sister used in her vision came back to me. *Someone with muscles.* As Jessie continued to pack up the various prizes and started the preliminary take-down of her booth, her biceps bulged. My sister had never said the killer was a man. Maybe it was a muscular woman.

"You notice the townspeople who come to the carnival and then hire people to steal from them, selling their antiques to make a big profit, don't you?" The third dart nudged a balloon, but the balloon didn't pop.

Jessie put down the boxes and walked slowly back over to the counter. With three darts left, and my mind solving the murder for me, I was in the zone.

"You realized someone stole the list and knew it could be matched up with things that had been stolen here and at your last stop, and had to quiet the guys who found out."

My aim was true on the next dart and it popped a balloon. Jessie stared at me like she wanted to murder me. My fifth dart went wide. Maybe I should run and find Aerie and Darla. I glanced behind me at the Ferris wheel, wondering if they were still stuck at the top. Suddenly, my plan didn't seem so smart. I tossed the last dart half-heartedly and was surprised by the popping sound.

"Two popped balloons. That's a live mouse." But her tone sounded more like she was thinking about stuffing me as a prize. She hustled behind the counter and handed me a cardboard box, which I automatically took. I backed away from the booth and tried to pull my phone out from the wristlet, but it was stuck.

Jessie was already around the counter with her arms full of stuffed animals, and a Bowie knife in her hand that she made sure I could see. "You're gonna come with me."

"No, I'm not," I told her.

"You don't think I could throw this like I threw the darts?"

This wasn't going like I had expected. I wanted to celebrate that I was right, that she had something to do with the murders. But with a sharp knife pointed at me, it was hard to congratulate myself. I nodded and agreed to go with her. I made a slight glance towards the Ferris wheel.

"Don't think your boy Tony is going to come and help you."

"Did Tony plan this whole thing?" I had to know.

"Tony?" She said his name with such irreverence that I suddenly felt better. "Tony couldn't find his way out of a paper bag." Jessie laughed a good long time over that. But she still carried a pile of stuffed animals with a knife hidden inside. She came close enough to hold the knife at my side. "Start walking."

"Where are we going?"

"Somewhere no one will see us. Now move."

She grabbed my elbow with a vice like grip. She marched me past the dart booth and the Ferris wheel.

17

Sweat trickled down my back as she pinched my elbow. The pile of stuffed animals smiled up at me from her arms where the Bowie knife was hidden.

My eyes frantically glanced from face-to-face and from ride to booth. Where could I run or find help? I didn't want to get anyone innocent involved. A group of kids ran past us bumping into Jessie. Two of the stuffed animals fell off the top; she gripped the remaining toys to keep the knife hidden.

In the second that she loosened her grip on my elbow, I yanked away from her and darted toward the closest food truck.

I pulled the door open to the cotton candy truck and climbed inside. I knew Jessie was in pursuit, so I ran to the front of the truck to make my way out the driver's side door. I stumbled climbing over the seats, almost dropping the box with my mouse in it. I didn't want to have to fess up to Aerie that I lost or injured our little friend. Jessie caught up and swiped at me with the knife, but I dodged as I opened the door. I practically fell out of the truck, landed on my feet, and sprinted across the grass. I wound my way around the fishbowl toss hopping onto the moving carousel. I didn't dare glance back. I worked my way around the prancing animals where little children sat. Once across I jumped down and continued running. The teacup ride gate was open; riders were getting into their seats. I pushed ahead of everyone and onto the platform. I took the chance to glance behind me. Jessie was within mere feet of catching me. She had lost all the stuffed animals and sheathed the knife, but she still had the look of death in her eyes. I had no doubt that she would strangle me if she got her hands on my neck. I ran between the teacups, as the ride controller shouted at me. Then I heard him shout at Jessie. "What's going on?"

She shouted back, "Mind your own business." Her heavy footfalls on the teacup platform followed close behind me as I pushed my way to the back toward the exit I had almost mistakenly taken when I was on the ride earlier. I held the mouse-box tightly and pushed the door open running for the woods. Jessie's footsteps stopped. She was detained by a coworker while she tried to explain the situation. I plunged into the woods. Running as fast as I could, deeper into the shelter of the trees. From what I remembered from the view on the Ferris wheel, Mr. Miller's farm lay on the other side of the woods. I just hoped I was running in a straight line. I took a second to orient myself. The probability of me running in a straight line was next to zero but I kept going anyway because I knew if Jessie found me, she would kill me.

I had been right that I couldn't run in a straight line. After what felt like an eternity, I realized I might be lost. I stopped and leaned breathlessly against a tree. I closed my eyes and listened to see if I could hear if Jessie had followed me. I heard muffled sounds coming from the carnival but nothing from the woods around me. I listened and looked around and tried to get my bearings. If I kept the carnival sounds to my back, I should come out on the Miller's property. I slowly picked my way across fallen trees and branches in the dense undergrowth of the forest floor. I didn't dare turn on my phone's flashlight but pushed through the tree branches with the mouse box as a shield. The trees thinned in front of me and I finally pushed out into an open field. Looking left to right, I saw that I was on the far end of the Miller property with the Miller house to my left.

Even though I hadn't heard her, I was still wary that Jessie might reach out and grab me from the secrecy of the woods. I walked further out into the field as I made my way toward the house. I realized two things as I dragged my exhausted body across the expanse of the Miller farm. One: that my legs were completely scratched up from running full force through the underbrush and, two: somewhere along the way I had lost my cell phone. The pretty purple clutch that Aerie had loaned me was no longer attached to my wrist. I shook my head. There wasn't anything I could do about it now. Hopefully, the Millers would be home and I could call Aerie's cell phone if my brain would calm down enough that I would remember the number. I climbed up on the porch and knocked on the front door. Mr. Miller answered, and I realized I must look worse than I thought. I noticed a twig sticking out of my hair and pulled it loose.

"Hi, Mr. Miller, it's Mira. Remember me from the diner?"

"Of course." He stopped staring and pushed the screen door open. "Come in, come in."

"Thank you." I stepped into the hallway of his farmhouse.

"Can I help you with anything? Have you been in the woods?"

I pulled a few more leaves from my hair. A scratch on my cheek burned.

"Are you okay?"

"I'm fine. But I seem to have lost my cell phone. I'm wondering if I can borrow your phone?" And then a thought occurred to me. "Mr. Miller?" He retrieved a phone from the kitchen. "Did you recently have something stolen?"

"I did. My grandfather's phonograph. That's all they took. I totally don't understand it but with the murders that happened, it's been very confusing."

"I think I might've seen that phonograph. Is it dark brown with a brass cone?"

"Yes, that's it. That's the one." Where did you see it?"

There was no hiding the fact now. Tony would be in trouble one way or the other. "In an RV near the carnival."

"I'll call Dan Lockheart. He'll know what to do." Before I could say anything, he was calling the police station.

I tried to sort out everything in my head, which was still spinning, and my lungs still ached from the run. Mr. Miller handed me a drink of water while I attempted to remember Aerie or Darla's phone numbers. Moments later Dan showed up knocking at Mr. Miller's front door.

"Ms. Michaels." Dan addressed me formally.

"Mira says she knows about the stolen phonograph."

"Mira, are you okay? Have you seen something?"

"Yes." I considered exactly what I should say. I needed to get back to the carnival, and to the RV and find out for myself. Something just didn't sit right. Not after Jessie's comment. I decided now was the time I had to throw Dan off the track. Just for now. "Dan, can you drive me home while I explain? I'm a little cut up and I want to disinfect these scratches, if you don't mind."

Detective Lockheart shifted gears and dropped out of his professional cool demeanor suddenly realizing that I was injured. "Of course, of course. Mr. Miller, if you'll excuse us. I'll keep you posted, thank you for calling."

Mr. Miller held the door for me. "Mira, I hope you feel better soon. Thank you for the information."

"No problem, Mr. Miller. I'll see you at the diner."

I walked out of Mr. Miller's house, down the steps and into Dan's waiting car. Surprisingly, it was a newer model and no longer that beat up vehicle that he had been driving for the last several months. Too bad. His old car had character, much like my Babs. But it was nice to slip into the leather seats with the air conditioning to cool me off. I sat with the mouse box on my lap, figuring out my next steps.

"You don't have to pretend, Mira. I know you're investigating the murders. I understand. Your sister is in town. I mean, her reputation precedes her in solving mysteries with the police in Massachusetts, but that doesn't mean any of this is safe." He obviously noticed my disheveled, scratched-up self.

I simply shrugged. He was right. But I wouldn't admit it.

"I also really want to apologize."

I held my breath.

"I shouldn't have agreed with your sister, about keeping an eye on you. You're an adult. You don't need me to watch over you." There was a nervously long pause. I didn't say anything.

"It's just that I..." Another pause.

"I care about you. And I don't want to see you get hurt." The words rushed out of his mouth.

"Oh," I said before even realizing it. The fact that he cared about me was a bit surprising. "I have problems with my sister getting involved in my life. That's why I moved here."

"I realize that now. And I'm really sorry." He turned on to Market Street. "Truce?"

I grinned at his goofy use of the word truce. But I nodded. "Truce." He pulled up in front of my house. "Is it okay if I call you to tell you about what I saw regarding the phonograph?"

He gave me a hesitant look.

"I think someone might be getting set up."

"Mira..."

"If I promise not to do anything reckless..." He was about to interrupt me. "Can you trust me to do the right thing?" He paused and I hurried the rest of what I needed to add, "I just can't implicate someone who is innocent. I've seen what damage that can do." I thought back to when the town thought someone had been poisoned in our diner. Nobody except Mrs. Orsa came in for a while and Aerie almost lost her business.

"I trust you. And I said I'd let you take care of yourself. But you know that I just want to make sure you don't get hurt." He sighed. "But if you put yourself in danger..." He ran his hands through his hair. "I just couldn't live with that."

"I'll promise to be more careful." This was truth. I needed to be better prepared so I wouldn't be so easily caught off guard. "And look." I waved at my house. "I'm going inside to clean up and get some rest. No danger."

He nodded. Resigned. "Go ahead, take care of yourself

and your scratches. We'll talk later." He gave me a smile that made me feel just a little bit guilty that I was lying through my teeth about going into the house and cleaning up and going to bed. I had to get back to the carnival and sort this thing out.

18

I walked up to my front door, keeping an eye on Dan as he pulled away and down the street. I was grateful he didn't actually wait until I went inside. Although, there was still the possibility that he might go back to the carnival. Knowing that it was closing tomorrow morning, he might insist on interviewing more of the carnival employees. I wanted to change into clothes that would hide the scratches on my arms and legs, but time was running out, and I had to get back and find Darla and Aerie, and explain what was going on.

I took one of the side streets up the hill toward the high school. And found myself behind the haunted house. I looked up and saw the stairs that led to the platform Tony had shown me. I could get a bird's eye view of the carnival grounds. I climbed the fire escape at the back of the haunted house and peered over the top.

I couldn't pinpoint Jessie anywhere. It was possible she was at her booth, which had its back toward me. I knew I'd have to avoid that area at all costs.

Then I spotted Aerie and Darla who were obviously

searching for me. I had to let them know I was okay, and I realized I could use their help.

Aerie noticed me as I stumbled across the cabling between booths. "Oh my gosh, are you okay?"

Darla examined my bruises carefully. "What happened?"

I brushed them both off. "Aerie, I lost your clutch, sorry. Jessie is involved. She pulled a knife on me."

Darla appeared shocked. "My visions are definitely not working."

"I'm fine. Listen, I think she and her accomplice are setting up Tony, so we have to get back." I suddenly noticed my fist still gripped the handle on the cardboard box. "I also won a mouse."

"You saved one?" Aerie took the box from me.

I held my breath as she peeked in the box. I figured it was a fifty-fifty chance it survived the run for our lives. I was still a little astonished I survived it.

Aerie squealed with delight. "Two mice! You saved two mice."

I could only imagine what Arnold would say about new little sister and brother mice in the house. "Aerie, you might have to keep those two."

I rubbed at the scratch on my cheek. "We don't have much time. Jessie has a knife and will use it. Can you guys go find Tony and make sure he's okay? I have an idea who might be behind this whole thing." I looked further across and saw the RV where Tony had taken me. That's where I was headed because if it wasn't Tony running the racket as Jessie had let slip, I had a sinking suspicion of who it might be.

"Are you sure it's not Tony?"

"I'm not sure of anything. If I'm wrong, and Tony is

involved, I want you to call Dan."

"Where are you going?" Darla surveyed the carnival. "We should stay together."

"There's no time." Even as I said it, lights began to blink off and people moved to the exits. "We need the cover of the crowd to make sure we're all safe." I suddenly thought it was a bad move that I hadn't involved Dan. But if he arrested the wrong person, and the rest of the carnival left, the real murderers could get away.

I used the same argument on Darla. "Trust me. Remember you said you wouldn't run my life anymore and you would trust my decisions."

There really wasn't time to waste, and I didn't want my best friend or my sister anywhere near Jessie or her knife. It was my turn to be the protective one. Which made me understand my sister and her protectiveness toward me a little bit better. Without waiting for an answer, I jogged toward the RVs and shouted over my shoulder. "Be careful!"

I made a wide circle to avoid the dart booth and came up alongside the ticket booth. I didn't look back but trusted that Aerie and Darla were doing their part in the plan. I might need Tony's muscle in a minute. Granny was not in the booth. It was closed for the evening. I knew where she would be. I cut across the field behind the ticket booth to the RV and, without knocking, pulled open the door.

The lights were on. Granny stood inside packing things into an overhead bin. She turned when I entered. Her face changed from grim determination to a lighthearted smile, but there was a hardness around her mouth. "Hello, young lady. Mira, isn't it?"

"Yes."

"Come in, come in. No one can say I'm a bad host."

I hesitantly took the step up into the RV but stood near

the door with my hand on the handle, ready to leave the second she did anything threatening. Although I had to say, the only thing threatening about the little old lady was her demeanor.

Suddenly, the door was yanked open. Because I held the handle so tightly I was pulled back and almost fell. Jessie pushed her way into the RV.

Granny's saccharine sweetness disappeared. "Where have you been?" she shouted at Jessie, who looked surprised to see me.

"Chasing this one across the grounds." She grabbed my upper arm, pinching my tricep mercilessly.

Right about now was when I really wished I had listened to Darla. My only consolation is that now I knew Tony hadn't had anything to do with it. Or at least there was enough evidence between these two to make it easier for me to believe that Tony was innocent of the murders. Jessie shoved me deeper into the RV living space. Granny was boxing up the phonograph.

"I'm still trying to figure out if you're a smart cookie or if you're dumb as a stump." Granny stayed focused on her task as she spoke. I wasn't sure if she was talking to me or to Jessie.

"Tony was quite taken with you. It's too bad that curiosity often kills the cat." She finished taping closed the box. And turned to Jessie. "Take her back in those woods. Get rid of her." The tone Granny used with that phrase let me know she was never the kind of granny that baked cookies.

Jessie nodded slightly and yanked my arm toward the door. At that moment it opened, and I could see the outline of Tony against the carnival lights.

"Mira! What's this about?" He wasn't surprised to see

me. Darla and Aerie stood behind him in the field. When I didn't move toward him, he stepped up into the RV. The space was now comically tight with the four of us in three square feet of space. He noticed how hard Jessie was gripping my arm. He shot a look at his grandmother. "What's going on?"

"I'm taking care of business. Something that you don't have the nerve to do."

"What are you talking about?"

"It's not your worry, Tony. Let me clean this up and we can move on to the next town. Don't worry your pretty little head about it."

"What do you mean 'clean this up'? What are you doing with Mira?" He grabbed Jessie's wrist as she held my arm. Jessie pulled back her arm and sent a right hook to his impeccable jawline. His face snapped back. He staggered a bit but he still held Jessie's wrist. He straightened and I noticed a flash of anger in his eyes as he stared at her. "What have you been doing for my grandmother?"

"Everything you won't do. Sassy boy." Jessie's grin let me know she had a little bit of monster in her. And I wasn't surprised.

"Tony, I let you run the carnival and I let you keep your nose clean. But there are certain things that have to be taken care of if you want to stay in the business."

"Like what, Granny? Like Joel and Ray? What did they do to you?"

"They stole money from me. My money." She growled. "And I took care of it." She pointed a crooked finger at me. "Now she needs to disappear, and we can be on our way. And if it makes you feel better, you can forget this whole thing ever happened."

Suddenly, Tony grabbed my arm. In the same spot that

Jessie had been pinching it. His firm grip was warm but not entirely tender. I glanced up at his face. That anger was still there. And I was a little bit more than frightened.

"I'll take care of it," Tony said.

Granny turned to him, examined his face closely and grinned. "I'm glad to see you coming to your senses, boy." She reached into a canvas bag next to the box that held the phonograph and pulled out a small pistol. She gave Tony another discerning look and grabbed his hand not holding my arm and shoved the pistol into it. "Take her into the woods and finish it. Then come back and let's get out of here."

"Consider it done." The emotionless sound of Tony's voice frightened me more than the pistol in his hand.

He kicked open the RV door and pushed me in front of him. He showed Darla and Aerie the gun pointed squarely at me and motioned for them to walk in front of us. Darla nodded briskly and held Aerie's hand. This was it. I had been wrong about the guy I liked, and I was going to get my sister and best friend killed. It was all my fault. I looked around to see if anyone was nearby to help, but the field was desolate.

I could barely keep up with the pace he set. He half-dragged half-marched me across the back field toward the woods. As we entered into the trees, my ankles were scratched again by the thick underbrush. We came to a halt. I close my eyes tightly.

Now would be when Darla would say she told me so. I had really thought Tony was a good guy. But, yet again, I was wrong.

I hoped in the shadow of the forest, Darla and Aerie could see how sorry I was. And then I felt the cold steel of the pistol being forced into my hand. I jerked back and opened my eyes. The Tony I knew was back and his eyes held that same kindness that I knew before. "Take the gun," he insisted.

I was still in shock. "You're not going to kill us?"

"Who do you think I am?" He shook his head. "Don't answer. I never thought my grandmother would be like this. I don't know. Maybe I knew." He pinched the bridge of his nose. "Take the gun, please. Bring it to your cop friend. It's evidence, right?"

"It's evidence." I stared down at the gun that more than likely killed both Joel and Ray.

I looked up at Tony. "Thank you."

"What are you thanking me for? I would never hurt you. Or anybody."

"You guys okay?" I turned to Darla and Aerie.

Aerie pulled me and Darla into a hug.

Darla leaned her head in to rest on my head. "I can't believe my visions weren't more useful. I'm sorry. You were amazing at figuring this all out, Mira. Really."

Hearing the pride in my sister's voice almost made the threat of being killed by my date's grandmother worth it. Almost.

"I'm sorry Tony. Sorry about your grandmother." I stepped out of the hug and touched his arm.

He looked down at his feet. "She needs to go to jail. Make sure your friend gets the gun."

"I will." I stood on my tiptoes and kissed Tony on the cheek. "You're a good guy, Tony."

I pulled my sister and Aerie deeper into the woods. I didn't look back. But I heard Tony's footsteps moving in the opposite direction. I pulled back branches and climbed over fallen trees and I knew just where we would come out. Poor Mr. Miller would have to call the police again.

19

When Dan showed up on the Miller property for the second time, he just shook his head. "Didn't I leave you at your house no more than an hour ago?"

"I still had stuff to do," I told him.

Darla had made fast friends with Mr. Miller and was in the kitchen offering to read his tea leaves.

I handed Dan the pistol, but he didn't take it. He went to his car, retrieved an evidence bag, and came back with it open. I dropped the small gun inside, and he sealed it.

"Are you ever going to stop solving my cases for me?"

"Probably not." I explained to him everything that had happened.

"You need to be more careful. You can't keep putting yourself in jeopardy."

I sucked in a breath. "Please don't tell me what to do." Maybe it was better if we didn't date. This time I didn't want a ride home. I needed to walk.

I regretted that idea about halfway. The exhaustion caught up with me. I strung my hands around Darla's and

Aerie's waists. "There's nobody I'd rather solve a mystery with than you two."

"So, this is a regular occurrence for you guys?" Darla's tone was my least favorite. It was big-sister-playing-parent voice.

"Everything except being held at gunpoint. That was new," Aerie offered, helpfully.

"You solve crimes back home all the time. This isn't all that different."

"I work with the police. That's a big difference..." Darla started in on the same parental tirade. We neared the diner. Darla stopped short under a streetlamp and turned to face me straight on. "Look, I hate to think of you in danger. But my visions have been...inconsistent to say the least, and you figured this all out without any help. I'm not saying I won't worry. But I see you have supportive friends." She smiled warmly at Aerie. Darla pulled me in for a hug.

I wrapped my arms around her, glad we had this chance again. The hug lasted a long time. And when I finally let go, I said, "Let's get some ice cream."

Darla said she had one last reading to do. But Aerie was on board and we went over to the diner and unlocked the door.

20

———

Early the next morning I was stifling a yawn when Tony came into the diner. I had just handed Aerie a plate of hash browns fresh off the grill.

"Someone found your cell phone on the grounds." He handed me the purple wristlet that held my phone.

"Thank you. I thought I lost it in the woods."

He grinned broadly at me. "You're still wearing it."

"What?" Then I realized he meant the necklace he'd given me. "This? Hey, it wards off the evil eye. It hasn't let me down yet."

"We're about to head out. I just wanted to stop by and say thank you."

"Thank you?"

"I had a great time with you this week. Besides that, you helped clean up the carnival. It's my family's legacy and I'm going to keep it that way."

"I'm proud of you, Tony." Just as I was about to tiptoe and kissed him on the cheek again, he put a strong arm around my waist and gently kissed me on the lips. I closed my eyes and relaxed against him.

"Maybe I'll see you next year?"

I opened my eyes to him smiling down at me. I was still stunned from the awesome kiss.

"I don't mean you need to wait for me or anything like that. But I'd love to go on a date with you again next summer."

"Oh yeah, sure." I already knew it would be hard not to pine for Tony even after everything that had happened.

"All right then." He turned to go. "I'll see you next summer, Mira."

"Bye," I whispered. The bells jingled over the top of the door as Tony exited. I stood there, frozen for a minute.

Aerie stood nearby. "Well, that was hot." She fanned herself with her tiny whiteboard.

I cleared my throat. "Where am I? Oh, right, the diner." She and I both laughed.

Darla came in soon afterward. "Was that Tony I just saw leaving?"

Aerie giggled.

"Yeah, that was him. He thanked me for helping out."

"He did more than that," Aerie said under her breath.

Darla raised an eyebrow. "Oh? I'll leave that alone," she said. "Well, the Studebaker is all packed. I'm ready to head home. It was nice meeting you, Aerie." She pulled Aerie into a hug. "Think about that reading. I can come back anytime to do it. Or you and Jay can come and visit me."

"I'll think about it. Thank you!"

I wasn't sure what the reading was about, but trusted my sister that she had Aerie's best interests at heart. Trusting my sister? That was new.

Darla turned to me. "Thank you for having me, Mira."

"I'm glad you visited."

"You are?"

"Yes." I didn't elaborate. Just knowing your sister has your back regardless of what goes on in your life was important to remember. I had long forgiven her for talking with Dan. She was just looking out for me. Dan and I getting together was a whole other animal I wasn't willing to look at right now.

"Will you call on your way back? Let me know where you are?"

"You're actually asking me to call you?"

"Yeah, why not?"

Darla smirked. "Okay. Hey, one last thing. Can we talk in private?"

Confused, I answered, "Sure." We walked back into the kitchen.

"What's up?"

"I spoke with the ghost that lives in your house."

"You did?" Clara had been silent since the fire. I wondered what she had to say to Darla.

"She's a really sweet person, Mira. She needs your help."

"My help? Why not yours?"

"I can't help her. You're here. I know you can do it. You have some skills of your own."

"I do?"

"You do. Try talking to Clara every once in a while; see where it gets you. She's stuck here until everything is resolved. I know you can help."

"Okay?"

"Okay. I really need to get on the road. It's a long drive."

"Want me to pack you a falafel?"

"I would love it if you packed me a falafel."

I walked back into the kitchen and made Darla her favorite falafel. And wondered what she meant by Clara needing my help. But the adventures last night were exhausting, so we'd attack the problem of the ghost another day.

The bells rang on the door, and I heard Dan's voice ordering an egg sandwich. Against my will, my heart beat a little faster. I swore right then and there, I would not date Dan, no matter what. My cell buzzed on the counter. My sister already? But no, the text said, *Kittens born this morning. 3. All yours in 8 weeks.*

PREVIEW OF POTTERY AND PERPS

I tried to start my Buick again for the fourth time. "Come on, Babs." I nudged. But nothing happened. I stared at the long line at the farm stand. Mr. Miller called to me over the customers, "I can take you over to the diner, it's not a problem. I'll just close up for a bit."

"I'll call a tow, she'll need to get there eventually anyway." Even with the windows open the summer sun had cooked the air in the car. I climbed out and stood next to Babs. The summer sun was in its glory today. I searched my phone and came up with the town's only fix-it garage. I pushed call. It rang and rang. No answer.

I slumped against the car. Now what? I supposed I could call Jay to verify I had the correct number. It couldn't hurt.

"Mira?"

"Hey, Jay. I ran into some car trouble and I'm wondering if you can recommend a tow."

"Sure, it's the place in town. Jasper's Garage."

"I just called there. No one picked up."

"Do you want me to stop by and take you over to the diner?"

"No, it's all right."

"Are you sure? Devon is here and he can run things for me."

I remembered Devon from his help with the kitchen renovations. Nice kid. "I'll try calling again and if I have any problems I'll call you back, how's that?"

"Alright, sounds good I'll watch for your call. Good luck."

I called the garage again and after five rings, someone picked up. "Jasper's Garage. Jasper speaking."

"Hi, Jasper, my car is dead. Can I have a tow? I'm at Miller's farm stand."

"Yep, I'll send the tow." Jasper sounded busy and he was quick to hang up.

I had just bought four gallons of milk and six dozen eggs. I was beginning to worry about them in the heat of the car. Maybe I should move them back to the shade of Mr. Miller's stand.

But before I could open the back door the tow truck had arrived. I walked away from Babs to greet the driver. When he stepped out of the cab a jolt of recognition ran through me. Wyatt's blond hair was shorter now, but he still had the same dreamy dark blue eyes.

"I know you." He shook a finger at me. "Route 80? Or was it 287?"

"You bought me a new battery," was all that came out of my surprised mouth.

He gave Babs a concerned look "I hope it wasn't a bad one?"

"It's been running great. Thanks. But you had mentioned something about the alternator before." I stepped aside as he walked to the front of the Buick and opened the driver side door in one swift motion and unlatched the hood.

"It could be." He lifted the hood of the car in a single graceful arc and propped up the support bar.

"Do you want to try starting it?"

"Sure." I hopped behind the steering wheel and made certain the emergency brake was on and started the car. Or tried to. Babs only made a ticking sound.

"You can stop."

I turned off the ignition and got out of the car and walked to the front and stood next to him. He surveyed the engine block.

"Do you know what it is?" I asked.

"I'll test the battery, just to be sure, but I think it's the alternator. We can tow it back to Jasper's and take care of it for you."

"This time I can pay for it." I smiled.

"I don't doubt it." He grinned back. "Let's get this baby hooked up."

There were certain benefits to being in the middle of Miller's field. There was enough room to allow the tow truck to drive around Babs and roll back close enough so the winch could pull her up onto the flat bed.

The other benefit was the fresh lemonade that Mr. Miller handed to each of us once his customers had departed.

"Thanks Mr. Miller." The iced lemonade hit the spot.

I watched as Wyatt sipped his drink, remembering when we had first met. "I thought you worked up near the Philadelphia area." I said.

"I do. I did. I'm out here helping my cousin Jasper. He needed the help, so I figured I'd take in the scenery."

"It is definitely more quiet here."

"Do you like it?" He asked as if maybe he wasn't sure if he liked the quiet.

"Yes. Actually, I do." I took the last sip of my lemonade. "I work at the diner. You should stop by, I'll buy you some lunch." Perhaps I could convince him to stick around.

"I might just do that." He looked down at his empty cup. "Hey, were you able to find that guy that kidnapped the cat?"

"I did. Thanks to your trucker friend's help. We found him and returned the kitty to her owner."

"That's great to hear. I knew you wouldn't give up."

I grinned.

"Let's get your Buick over to Jasper and fix her up."

We thanked Mr. Miller for the drinks and walked back to the truck. Wyatt started the engine as I climbed into the passenger seat. I imagined finding fast food wrappers, chip bags or other garbage. Instead, what I found was very peaceful, extremely clean, detailed tow truck cab. In place of a pine tree deodorant hanging from the rearview a single crystal on a black silk cord caught the light from the early morning sun. I relaxed.

"I can't lie to you," Wyatt glanced at me as we turned onto the road, "an alternator is not cheap."

"I figured as much." Internally I cringed. Most of the money Alex had given me or rather returned to me, had already been paid out to Bob at the hardware store for the kitchen appliances. Not car troubles.

"I'll make sure Jasper gives it to you at cost."

"You don't have to do that Wyatt." I sighed. "I've got savings."

"Jasper and I can give your old girl a good once over and let you know if anything needs shoring up. More like a wellness check. This girl is pretty old. You might want to start thinking about investing in something newer."

I noticed he hadn't said new. "Does Jasper sell used cars?"

"He does. I could look into it for you?"

"I don't know. Babs and I have been through a lot."

"I hear you. I had an old clunker once too. Good times." He grinned to himself.

I mentioned the milk and the eggs were in the back seat and how they were needed at the diner. Wyatt offered so I handed him my keys and he dropped me off at the diner. He even helped me carry in the four gallons of milk. After he said goodbye Aerie gave me the raised eyebrow. "Who was that?"

MORE MIRA MICHAELS MYSTERIES

If you enjoyed this story and would like to read more about Mira and her lovable cat Arnold, check out more of the Mira Michaels Mysteries.

CATS AND CATNAPPING
KEYS AND CATASTROPHES
PRANKS AND POISON
CONSTRUCTION AND CALAMITY
CARNIVALS AND CORPSES
POTTERY AND PERPS
GABLES AND GRIEVANCES

Please consider writing a review on Amazon to let others know more about Mira's adventures, please don't share spoilers! Reviews help readers find these stories which helps writers like me. That way I can continue to write what I love and create more stories for you.

Thanks bunches,

Julia

SUBSCRIBE AND SAVE!

Simply go to Julia's website at www.juliakoty.com/subscribe and add your email to our mailing list. You'll be included in our exclusive club and be the first to learn about new releases and special deals on the stories you love.

www.ingramcontent.com/pod-product-compliance
Lightning Source LLC
Chambersburg PA
CBHW020821190726

48285CB00006B/2361